Alex Henry
George Grant's Metahuman's
No Man's Island

To my father
For always supporting me

Chapter One

You may not trust me, but everything I say is true. If you think humans are the strongest life forms on the planet, then you are not one of us. If you have the inept immune system and strength of a human, then you are not one of us, but if you sense power surging through your veins, you might be one of us. If something you suspect might have happened because of you that seems extraordinary, possibly, you might be one of us.

Look, I never agreed to be a Meta though. Don't think being a Meta is easy. My life is not. I didn't want this to happen. Being a Meta comes at a price. This is my story because I am a Metahuman.

I awoke to the sun blaring in my eyes. I lay on the grass, sprawled out. The humidity caused sweat to pour down my face. My hair felt as wet as swim trunks that had soaked in a pool. The lush grass on my hands felt like hundreds of slim needles poking at me. I tried to get up, but I felt lethargic. I planned on figuring everything out later and going back to sleep, so I closed my eyes. The sound of the surrounding objects was foreign. Nothing around me was familiar.

I looked at my arms, turning my hands back and forth in front of me. Prompted to get up, I did. After setting myself up, I slowly looked around. I assessed my situation, to remember, something, anything, but, my mind was a blank space. Questions flowed into my mind. I don't remember ever voyaging here, or in fact, anything in my past, except my name is George Grant. How did I get here?

I looked around, but there was no one in sight. Trash and debris washed up on the sandy beach. White rocks mixed in the sand tumbled in the wind, and into my eyes. There were groves of bulbous trees, blackberry bushes, and lush grass all around me.

Behind all of that, a large mountain sat. The mountain was made of gray and black granite that glistened. The sun reflecting off the mountain was almost blinding. The top of the mountain appeared red because of the sun.

While processing the gargantuan sight, out of the corner of my eye, I viewed a stream that flowed into a large pond, and that stretched out and fell into a waterfall. The water looked pure. To stand here felt foreign to me.

The clothes on me were teal Hurley denim shorts with a mixture of colored striped socks, and a light blue shirt. This situation made me feel frustrated. It bothered me that I was alone. Tears welled in my eyes, and I wiped the sweat from my face.

I yelled, "**Help, anyone. Please? Anyone?**" I needed to face the facts. No one was coming. I needed to help myself. I did not realize that I was walking. Remembering nothing about how I was on this island made me feel scared.

I felt a weight in my pocket. I reached into my pocket to see what this was. The smooth object was cold in my hands. I took the item out of my pocket. The object was precious and shiny in the sunlight. The item appeared to be a brass tree carving. It glistened in the sun as I held my new interest high. Branches twisted, and turned on it, and made up an amazing form.

My greatest possession I held in my hands, but where did it come from? The carving felt as precious as a rich man's gold. The carving somehow made me feel safe.
My throat was parched, and I had an empty stomach. I looked at the seawater, but I refused to drink saltwater.

A precious apple tree stood in a distance with abundant apples hanging down. I slowly walked to the apple-tree. The tree looked about 30 feet away, but it was much further than that. I sauntered towards the tree, and I felt as if I had not eaten in weeks. The tree came at an arch with green leaves. They looked rosy red and juicy.

I hopped up into the air and struggled to get to the first branch, but the lofty tree rose high over me.

I dashed toward the tree. I sprung off the trunk of the tree using the stiff trunk as a springboard. I grabbed the branch. I threw my legs up in the air and rested them on a branch. The tree-shaded me. The leaves with water on the tips dropped to the ground. My head drooped, and I held tight to the solid dark brown branch. I groaned and forced myself straight up. Next, I snatched a glowing, ripe apple, and twisted and distorted the branch, and the stem finally snapped.

I flipped the apple up in the air, immediately I dropped out of the tree. I plummeted to the ground and hit my right arm. "AAHH." My voice cracked as I shrieked. My arm ached. My heart thumped with a quick beat. I lay in the grass assessing what to do. Needing to find shelter and water was essential.

I took my brass tree carving out of my shorts pocket. I used the brass object to slice my apple. The rosy red apple was juicy. The juice only made me thirsty. I wondered how to survive. I got up and started to make a plan.

I wandered to the rim of the jungle. The jungle contained felled trees and fresh mud. The mud stuck to my shoes along with the crushed leaves in it. Leaves moved in the trees the afternoon was hot.

I understood, somehow, I knew how to make a hut. As I led off into the jungle, I saw some small wild pigs. I needed to search for a freshwater source soon. If I got disoriented in the jungle and needed to find safety, where would I go? Nothing made sense.

I collected wood. This wood needed to be stocky and dry. Unluckily, everything was wet.

Anger grew in me. Almost everything made me angry. My thoughts made me angry. My weak arms made me angry. The parched throat I bore was causing anger.

I ventured into the jungle grabbing small sticks. I found four big long branches to be the main base of the structure. I lugged the branches over my shoulder. There were bruises almost everywhere on me for some reason. It was if I recently was beaten.

I took a minute to collect a breath on the crushed leaves. I could sense the birds in the air. I heard the plants shaking. The wind blew with a whistling. Crickets chirped in the distance. Animals scurried on dead leaves. Branches dropped off of trees. The stream made a soothing sound as water moved through the rocks

Then, I heard a large crash with a shriek. The sound made me jump. An animal was now shrieking continuously.

I hid out of fear, but I was also curious. I tried to locate where the noise came from. There were animals scurrying up trees and into the forest. They were silent as they escaped. I searched for the source of the sound.

I was scared, alone, and hopeless. I got lost in my thoughts.

I decided to rest on a log. The log was wet, but I did not care. My throat felt dry. My hope left me. Suddenly there was a shriek. The sound was very close.

I looked around. Trapped under a large brown rough log was a small, wild pig. The tree had fallen, and the pig's tail was trapped. The tree had been cracked in half.

The piggy was brown and pink. I could use it for food, but I saw it was helpless. I put my small hands on the rough edges of the log and tried to move it. The log was large and would be heavy. I felt sorry for the pig. I whispered, "One, two, **Three.**"

Using all my might, I used one hand to push the rough, brown, broken log up, while I pulled it free. The log lifted just enough to set it free. The pig had smooth skin that brushed against me.

It had a reddish-brown nose and smelled terrible. I plugged my nose. The odor made me want to vomit. Soon, the pig jumped from my arms and scampered away squealing.

The long log dropped, and I jumped back just in time. The log made a huge noise when it hit the ground. I hopped back, as it kicked dust into the air. The dust got into my eyes making them burn, and I covered my mouth with my shirt and walked away coughing.

I grabbed a long log and put it on my shoulder before I left. I also grabbed some shorter limbs that fell off the tree. The big log strained my strength. The log weighed almost as much as I did. I walked through the jungle, back to the sandy beach.

The log felt wet. It made water wrinkles on my skin. As I walked, the smooth grains of sand made crunching sounds.

When I got to the apple tree, I placed the three limbs I held against the tree. They would act as my largest posts. In between two of the apple trees, I put my biggest and longest log. I set logs and branches in between the two trunks so they would never fall. It was sturdy and rigid as a stone

I continued working. I collected many small twigs and branches. It took hours to gather all the wood and set it into the main structure. Eventually, it took shape and was something that would give me shelter.

I started collecting leaves. All the leaves I found, either fell off a tree, or the leaves lay dead. I piled these leaves onto the hut. This covered my hut completely, and rain would not get through easily.

I sat down to assess my situation. Why am I here? I knew my name, and that's the only information I had. I must have been in a coma or blacked out. Maybe I was knocked out and forgot my past. Maybe I had amnesia. How did I end up on this island? Had I floated across the sea? There was nothing that helped me understand. Nothing washed up on the shore. Did someone just throw me away? I was so confused.

For the rest of the day I fidgeted. It bored me that there was not much to do. The air slowly cooled, and I began to feel better

I mounded up a pile of sand. This mound was as big as a king's throne. I ran and leaped into this massive mound of smooth-grained sand. The grains of sand felt soft against my face.

I felt free for a moment, but I soon felt the despair return. I felt like a lost soul, lonely, and afraid. I was entirely alone.

The only connection I had had while I was here was with a smelly, fat pig. It wasn't anything I could talk to, but it was the closest thing I had to a companion.

I spent my time climbing onto green lush trees and jump off into the sand. I would get tired, rest, and then go do it again. All I had to eat were the juicy apples. The day was long. I had no one to talk to. I didn't feel crazy when I talked to myself, because that's all I could do.

The sky soon grew dark, and I got in my hut and rested. Before going to sleep, the fact occurred to me that life would be harder than today. I couldn't live this way for very long. There would be dangers, and I had to learn better survival skills. I had to make a better fortification.

These thoughts made it hard to sleep, but I had to sleep. I needed energy for whatever would come at me tomorrow. Soon, I closed my eyes, and I drifted off to sleep.

I opened my eyes to the sun glaring at me. I stretched my arms. I heard a noise emitting from outside the shelter. I realized **I'm not alone.**

Chapter Two

I walked toward the sound. "Is anyone there?" whoever or whatever was outside the shelter inquired. I rushed out of my shelter and asked, "Who's there?" I stepped towards the voice. I was so excited and scared. I almost wanted to crumple up into a ball and suck my thumb. Whatever was behind my hut couldn't compare to being stranded on an island by yourself. I stood tall, and I turned to face the other side of my oval-shaped hut.

Right in front of me were seven kids. Some kids looked pale and looked as if they would not make it much longer on this island. Some looked capable and strong.

I was shocked to see anyone else on this island. I stood staring every kid down for a quite a length of time. The kids in front of me must have thought I was a freak. I couldn't speak, but then I got the words out, "What, what, what, how, when?" I stuttered.

There was a kid in muddy clothes, but his shirt was black, and his shorts were gray. He wore socks that were long. The boy had the most frisky, blackish/brown hair, and was standing to the left of everyone. He exclaimed with his head down, "My name is Christian, uhm, but you can call me Chris. I'm 12. We crashed here on this island a few days ago. We are the only survivors. All our supplies got destroyed in the crash. No adults survived. There's no tools or supplies?"

I stared at the boy with a dead-faced look. "Okay slow down there Chris. My name is Jack. So glad to meet anyone else here" asserted a boy with silky, glimmering blond surfer hair. He wore a red Hurley shirt with blue school shorts. He also had on black Nike socks. He looked around two to three years older than me because of his height. His eyes were blue as the ocean

A redhead girl with a red baseball hat stood silent and said nothing. The girl looked Hispanic and had serious sunburn on her. She had on a button up with red and white checkers. Her pants had holes in them with a faded out blue color. She looked timid. She appeared as if she were many years older than me.

There was a kid with a blue button up and fancy black and gray stitched pants. He wore a stylish pattern on them. "How do you do? My name is Arthur, and I am happy to meet you. I am fifteen," he exclaimed.

There was another girl with brown silky hair that was curly and dirty. She had red polyester shorts and a shirt saying fitness on it. She didn't look like someone that was athletic. The girl said, "My name is Chloe."

There was a boy that was wearing a blue shirt with a football in the middle. He had on nice polyester gray shorts. His hair was thick and brown. He had a large grin on his face that said something like I know what I am doing here, being stranded is no problem. He informed, "My name is Christian, um what was your name again?"

I stuttered for a second, then I took a deep breath in, and I vocalized, "My name I think is um, George. I don't really know my age. I don't remember how I got to this island, or well, well anything in my past, really."

Chloe stated, "You look like you are twelve or thirteen. How could you possibly not remember anything? You are joking. How ironic is that Jack?" she asked as she laughed.

"Shut up Chloe," Jack snapped. Chloe stopped laughing. She stood tall. Chloe looked as if she was afraid.

"I really don't remember. I know how to speak, and everything. I know how to do things, but I don't remember my life."

Chloe chuckled, "Yeah. You must have memory loss of some sort, or maybe you had one of the biggest concussions known to man. You seem smart enough, maybe you had a concussion?"

I was getting frustrated. All these questions, but so little answers. Jack walked towards me and said, "Well another problem for another time. We need to eat or make a shelter or do something. Preferably anything other than this."

I was happy that Jack was sticking up for me. Chloe inquired, "Why can't we talk about this? This subject is the most interesting thing we have talked about the entire time we have been here. He doesn't mind it."

Jack turned to her and said, "Stop picking on him. I know how it feels to not know about your past. I don't remember mine either. You should try waking up, and people picking on you because you can't remember anything."

It was nice to have someone defend me, and he didn't know me. Chloe's chin quivered, and her face changed from a wide grin to a fretted frown.

"Guys, I don't want to cause a fight. I feel a little uncomfortable talking about that. I was asking myself all the same questions, so I can understand why you asked me that," I responded.

"Well, now that we found one, what do we do?" asked Christopher in a meager voice. "Did you guys come all this way just to see if there were any others stranded?" I requested.

"Yeah, we were hoping for an adult too, but we got you," Chloe stammered cantankerously.

I responded, "Oh I'm sorry that there aren't adults here, but what more information would an adult have than a whole group of kids could have? If I had to choose between having one adult and a group of kids, then I would choose a group of kids."

Jack rejoined, "Do you have any food, or have you found any? We are all starving, and we're super tired. I think that's what's making us grouchy."

"Over there," I responded pointing towards the apple tree next to us. They must have been hungry, because if he couldn't see the apple tree sitting five feet away from him, then he had no energy at all.

Jack walked towards the apple tree and climbed up. He tossed apples down to everyone. The kids stared at their apples like it was the holy grail. We all ate and sat on the sand. None of us spoke.

After sitting for a while, I got up, and Christopher followed. Christopher explained, "I know we are all tired, but we need to build a shelter or a few of them. If something were to happen it would come in handy to have it."

"Wait, but we can't live on the beach. We need to build in the jungle. We can't live off of apples, and saltwater for the rest of our life. We have to move tomorrow, because I want to build one big shelter, like, like, like a treehouse. Treehouses would be great in the hemlock part of the jungle. I was a builder as a kid. Not to brag though, just putting it out there. There is a large groove of them about three miles towards the center of the island. We get a day of rest, we build a temporary home, and leave tomorrow."

(Chris really knows what he's doing), I thought. Almost everyone moaned. After getting up, everyone looked for things we could bring with us. After everyone had left to scavenge, Jack leaned over. He informed, "Hey don't worry about the stuff these kids say. Usually, they're just hungry and are upset that they are in this situation." He patted my back, then started off.

"Thanks," I stated, but he was already on his way.

I walked around, admiring the work the kids were doing. I helped with carrying material and organizing our stash.

After we worked for a while, I decided to test out a new idea. Walking towards the seashore, I took my socks off and walked over to some dirt. I took out my brass tree carving, I banged on the dirt, loosening up a patch. I grabbed the dirt and put it into my sock. I put more, and more into my socks until they were full, then I walked towards the calm watered seashore.

As I stepped into the waters, the sand on my feet was smooth, and my feet felt great in the calm waters. I dunked my socks into the water and let them get soaked. Soon, my dirt was mud. I walked back over to the unfinished fort and I tossed the mud on top.

The fort sat far enough from the ocean that the waves wouldn't be able to reach it. The fort was large enough for everyone.

They stuck a humongous log bigger than the one I had put in my fort deep in the ground. It was almost as tall as the apple trees. They built the rest of the fort like a teepee, but it was more of a half oval shape. My hypothesis was that when the mud dries it would stick the wood together and do the same job the leaves do. I did this over and over until we started to run out of light.

Soon, everyone had climbed into the half oval shaped hut. Everyone was tired and sweat poured down their face. They all sagged to the floor and tried to relax.

I walked toward the hut, as tired and lethargic as the rest of them. I walked through the entryway into the hut. The entry had a long-extended arch. I had to bend down to get through, but once inside I couldn't even jump, and touch the ceiling. The arch was smooth and dark brown.
Everyone lay in the cool hut. The air was much warmer outside, but the coolness felt great. I sat down and rested.

Everyone took some time to rest, but soon we started to play. Christian showed us how he could juggle, with a few apples. Chloe bragged about how she was a genius, but after Arthur tested her with some questions, she changed the topic.

To have friends with me felt amazing. Before I felt lonely. I could actually relate to what their experiences were.

Soon, the sun was setting, and the temperature dropped. The sky was a pink and yellow color. It was beautiful. Chris informed, "I am gonna get a fire started if that's okay. Could you guys help me get a few sticks and brush?"

I replied, "Absolutely."

Chris stated, "Just remember, only get dry wood, and dead yellow grass is great for burning."

I added, "Yeah I think I know what burns. I think I got this."

"Okay," Chris said, "I mean you were just born like yesterday."

"Whatever," I responded. I got up as everyone did. I looked around for anything dead, and in the distance, a dead tree sat up on a mound. The dead tree appeared as if it got enough water and sunlight, but even from a distance, one could see the large termite holes that covered the trunk. I decided that that was a good place to collect.

As I walked in that direction, I could see the sky. I never paid much attention to the beauty of the sky before. While gazing at the sunset, the clouds turned to a pink, blue and orange color. The sky shone bright, and on this cold deserted island, I finally felt at ease.

As I walked up the mound, gazing at the sky. I wasn't looking where I was going. I kicked a large rock as I started up the hill. I tripped, flailing my arms. I hit my knee first, then my face. When my knee hit the ground, it scraped against a pointed piece of bark.

I laid there and looked at the gashes on my leg. I moved my hair from my eyes to check the wounds. I got back up and got my balance, then I limped over to the tree.

I grabbed a loose dead branch and shook it rapidly. The tree crackled, and the entire thing shook. The branch broke loose and fell to the ground. I picked up a few pieces of dead, yellow grass and shoved them in my pockets. I hobbled my way back to the fire pit.

There was a neat pile of wood and dead, yellow, grass. I threw down what I had collected for the fire. I limped over to where all the others were.

Chris brought dry grass, and Jack had some large sticks. Chris was attempting to light the fire. He was rubbing one long stick with a rock under it and another short stick. He had been rubbing these sticks together for a while.

There were three pillows, and three blankets set out in different areas. I sat down by Jack and Christopher. These two were laughing when I sat down. They continued cracking jokes as I turned on my side. I asked Christopher, politely, "I know this might seem impertinent, but why did the plane crash?"

His brown eyes watered, and he replied hastily, "My family was going on a vacation to South America, a surprise from my dad. In the middle of our flight, there was an unexpected lightning storm. Lightning hit the cockpit, mid-flight. The glass shattered and killed the two pilots. No one knew how to operate the plane. It crashed landed on the island. The men and women all let the children out first. Most of the kids were killed in the crash. The plane exploded again, as we were getting out and killed everyone inside." He was now sobbing.

I asked, "Where is the plane on the island?"

Jack replied, "A few miles in toward the center of the island, like where Chris was talking about. Around the grove of hemlocks. That's where I met them."

We talked and got to know each other. We had a lot of the same interests. Soon, the fire started, and Chris sat down by us.

As the night drifted on, I couldn't follow what everyone was talking about, because I was so tired. When they asked me a question, I couldn't understand what they had said. I didn't **worry about** getting into the hut to sleep in case of a storm. I closed my eyes and drifted off to sleep.

Chapter Three

I woke up to tapping on my arm. As I lay there, the tapping got more intense. I rolled over and opened my eyes. I jumped to my feet, ready to fight.

"Woe, woe, wait, just a second ago you were out cold. Now you look like you're gonna box," Chris exclaimed with a grin on his face. The temperature was cold. I could see my breath on the air. Jack was in the tent, and Chris was waiting for me. "How are you doing sleeping beauty? Everyone's waiting," proclaimed Chris.

"Shut up," I replied. Jack led me out of the tent. Everyone was up, and they were all ready to go. The shy girl (as I called her) had her gray backpack on. The backpack looked full. "Ready, everyone?" asked Christopher.

"Yep," replied Jack. We started off into the shaded, lush jungle. I thought to myself. I didn't know what was in this jungle. Did Chris really know what he was doing? I don't know. Even if we get to the hemlocks, how can we build a treehouse able to hold all of us? What if there are termites? If we don't build it correctly, it might collapse, and people could get killed. There are no doctors here.

These unanswered questions overwhelmed me, but I tried to pull myself together. I tried to put these thoughts out of my mind. I knew that my new life would not be all sunshine and rainbows.

I didn't feel very energetic, but I couldn't bear seeing the shy girl haul our utilities. I walked up to her, and I asked, "Hey you want me to carry that?"

"Sure thanks. That is so nice of you."

"Oh, no problem. We can't have only one person carrying the team."

"Um, my name is Alice. Sorry if I didn't talk a lot before, I was just so overwhelmed. You know," she replied.

"Oh, it's no problem, and we're all overwhelmed," I said. She lowered the backpack from her shoulders and gave it to me.

When I put the gray backpack on my back, it felt like an extra body I had to drag. The backpack felt like a million pounds. My back hunched. I tried to lift with my legs. We headed off into the forest.

The rainforest was lush but walking into an unknown land was scary. The trees stood up tall, and critters crawled everywhere. The rainforest was beautiful.

Chris walked with pride, face up high. He had a perfect posture and no slouch. Everyone else was very jittery though. I wanted to curl go somewhere safe. Home! The island was cold, and in the rainforest, it was colder. Trees shaded us.

Not much sunlight broke through. My arms shook. My legs buckled. The hairs on my legs stuck up.

Time passed in pure silence. Finally, I got the guts to ask questions, I was dying to ask, "How long have you guys been here?"

"Roughly three days," Chris replied sternly.

Chris then had a grin on his face, and stated, "You know, this forest kind of reminds me of a book I read called The Hobbit. When the characters are in the jungle, these giant spider things bigger than humans jump out. They capture them and try to feast upon them. Then."

"*Shut up Chris*!" Arthur ordered.

"Oh, are my cool stories scaring you, tough guy," Chris joked.

"No!" Arthur muttered back, but then went on with a scared look on his face. He glared at the forest. I laughed.

"Oh, you want me to rip you a new one too!" Arthur threatened.

"Oh wow, wow! I don't think I could compete with you, but you should be careful you look pretty tasty?" I mocked. That shut Arthur up, and I smiled.

After hours of walking, Chloe moaned, "I'm hungry! I can't take it anymore. I'm tired of eating apples. Can't we find some meat."

I told her, "We will get some later, okay." We continued to walk and walk. The moaning and obnoxiousness of these teenagers irritated me. Everyone was quiet, and I was okay with that. My bones felt like jelly, and my legs were about to give out.

"Okay, I am sitting down. You guys suck," Chloe declared. I didn't complain. We took a rest and ate an apple that now tasted bitter. Having apples so many times, made me hate their taste.

We started to talk. Chris told us how we would make the treehouse, which got my brain spinning. They told me about their walk to the seashore, and how they came across multiple dead skunks. (I have to be careful of what I say), I thought to myself. "What was home life like back when, well, you know?" I gestured.

Chris spoke, "Well, my town was small. Roughly about thirty thousand. People there were hard working. I had a lot of responsibility. We lived in the country. I built and played sports in my free time. The town itself was nice and had lots of restaurants. People, there are very kind."

"It sounds nice," I replied.

Chloe shrugged, "Enough about Chris, let's talk about me. My dad was super rich, and it was awesome other than him being gone all the time. My servants picked up after me. It was amazing. I lived on a street with other rich people. My Mom was always helping, I mean was, I mean…. Um… Um, next person please."

"What about you Alice?" I asked.

Alice replied, "Oh, well I lived in a town of six-thousand, so tiny, but the people were so kind and nice. Our schools were great, and we had a great time with our teachers. I had a few friends. I would rather have a few friends that I would get to know really well, rather than having a ton of friends I wouldn't know as well. The town was modest. Our home was an average size with a two-acre lawn. I have two nice older brothers. I miss everyone." I wanted to ask something like, well what were your parents like, but I restrained myself.

Everyone went around talking about home life, and by the end, they all had tears streaming down their faces except me and Jack.

We were in a very thick grove of trees, and it was getting dark quickly. All the lights that shone in earlier were mostly gone. In the darkness, I could barely see, but the light was still good enough to continue on the trail.

As we walked through the jungle, we decided to all take a second to just breathe. I sat down on a small log. The log was flat enough to sit on.

As I admired the jungle, I realized we were missing one person. It was Arthur. He had disappeared, and no one had noticed that he left. (We were not very alert. What if something took him?). The wind made the bushes sway. I was in full alert.

Then I heard something jump out of the bushes. **"We are all gonna die!"** someone hollered. I sprung up with my fists out, ready to fight. As I peered toward the bushes, I saw Arthur. He was trying to scare us. Chloe was the only one unaffected by the prank.

Arthur laughed at all of us. He pointed at us calling us names. I had the urge to punch him. The more I got to know him, the less I liked him.

We kept walking through the forest. It was a grueling trial and my body got more lethargic by the second. I put the back of my hand on my forehead and wiped the sweat away. I looked forward. Hopefully whatever lay ahead would be better than where we were.

Chapter Four

As we got closer to our destination, cranberry bushes and lush green grass filled the forest. Trees of every kind spotted the forest. In the jungle, Coniferous tree, Hawthorns, Palms and many others almost blacked out the sky.

A stream flowed in a distance. The stream was full of clear, fresh water, flowing through the rocks. I ran towards the stream, with my throat as dry as a cactus.

I jumped into the stream and held my dirty hands in a cuplike shape. I brought them up to my mouth and gulped the water. The water was so refreshing.

The water in my mouth was almost as amazing as finding other people on the island. My brown hair was now soaked, but the water was so satisfying. I drank more. Finally, I walked up the mound, drenched from my shoes up to the bottom of my peach colored shorts.

Everyone gave me the, are you crazy, look. I ignored it. "What are you looking at?" I asked. Even though people flashed weird looks, they all eventually did the same thing, except Arthur. All I had eaten since the trip started was apples, and I had found no water. Arthur exclaimed, "I'm not having that filthy stream water."

Chris said, "Ok rich boy, whatever." A tiny stick dropped off of an Arborvitae tree and hit Arthur in the head only seconds later. He turned and kicked the tree with a thick, dark, brown trunk. He screamed, "OOWW!" with eyes of rage. Arthur looked like he would cry, but he held his tears. Chris exclaimed, "Karma."

"Shut up!" Arthur hollered. I laughed.

Chloe moaned again, "Why can't we stop here and rest?"

"For the last time, can you shut up?" Christopher moaned. Everyone walked into a sandy area, in the center of a grove of trees. We all got in a circle right by a large Arborvitae tree.

Then, Alice shouted, "Are we all a bunch of babies? All we do is argue."

"Yeah guys," Chloe stated.

"And you have been the worst of all," Alice declared, pointing to Chloe.

Chris stated, "Wait, I think we are close. Look ahead. Do you see all the trees destroyed from the plane crash? See how the plane slid across the jungle, destroying the trees."

I could see the trees that fell in a big line, as if the plane had ridden on top of the trees, like a surfboard, as it broke through the trees and fell to the ground.

There was a slight breeze brewing. A broad blackberry bush wall beside us swayed. There was an opening in the wall. It seemed like a mini maze but made of natural plants and objects. The blackberry bushes were poky and green. "This is for sure the way we came," Christopher spoke.

"That means we are close," Arthur stated.

"Let's get going," I implored. As the straight path we were following was covered in blackberry bushes. We kept walking. Everyone had been silent since the bickering stopped. We all needed time to think.

Christopher eventually spoke, "My parents died in a car crash when I was three. My foster parents never pay attention. They would fly me out to my aunt and uncles, and then they would go on vacations without me. My foster parents are slobs, and I always have to cook meals. I am expected to walk to the supermarket and get groceries." This story shocked me. "How about you Arthur?" I asked.

"Shut up!" Arthur demanded. Before I could ask anyone else about their life, we came up to a huge wall of blackberry bushes. There was a path through it, though. Chloe said, "This is the path we took, I think."

We started through the blackberry bushes. We walked for what seemed to be forever. We turned every which way, and it seemed like we must have been going in circles. Soon, enough, we came upon a large ditch. After spending a long moment, gazing at this ditch with rocks of all colors, I realized it must have been a stream in the past.

A big rock that lay to my right was at least four times my size. This rock was gray with speckles of white. The white parts of the rock looked like crystals. The rock was eroded on the side.

This ditch crossed under the bushes to my right. The bushes that were lush, scraped me as we walked through them. I helped everyone get down into the ditch then back out. I was the last person out of the ditch. We walked in between the blackberry bush walls. The weather got colder and windy. I wished I had a warm coat on.

Alice unzipped her gray backpack. She grabbed a thick, gray jacket, with a fluffy inside. She draped it on herself.

I was rubbing my hands as fast as I could against my arms to try anything to stay warm. I was jealous and angry that Alice was warm and had only one coat. I knew she didn't expect this scenario when she packed. "Do you have any other coats?" Chloe asked Alice.

"Sorry, but no," Alice replied.

"Are you serious?" Christopher moaned

"Am I supposed to have all the supplies in the world? Not to mention I didn't know I would be on a deserted island," Alice stated, unwilling to lend her warm coat to anyone else.

As we were walking, and I hit my shoulder against the side of a tree. "Smooth," Chloe said. I chuckled.

Then I heard a rumbling noise in the bushes. A rumbling sound came from behind the bushes. I stared, to see what was behind this blackberry bush. The dead bushes rumbled and shook. I couldn't see what was on the other side, but for sure it wasn't good. I could see nothing, but blackberry bush vines.

I picked up a dark, brown, pine cone from below a tree, and I tossed it at an arch over the tall bush. I could tell it hit something rather than the ground because it made a *thud*. There was something behind there but what?

I bent down and glared through the giant bush. I stood back up. I still couldn't see anything. The leaves and thorns made up a huge, thick layer.

Soon, two curvy, brown, longhorns poked out of the bush. I impulsively walked over to the bushes and put my hands on one of the horns. The horns were strong and smooth. They looked like but no, it couldn't be, I thought. Before I could warn the others, something terrifying happened. The beast jumped out of the bushes. The huge black thing threw me back and sped at me. It had thick, black hooves with mounds of fluffy hair. Its belly was enormous but strong. It was massive, and we didn't know what to do.

The beast knocked me down again with its' horns. I smashed, face first into the dirt. My arms flailed on the rocks and dirt. My head bounced against the ground, then came back up. It felt like my teeth were vibrating.

This animal was a buffalo, and I had pissed it off.

The horns smashed into my gut once again. It was the most excruciating pain in my memory. I shot into the air, then plummeted to the ground. I skidded across the dirt and the rocks. I collapsed to the ground. Everything went blurry. I started to breathe fast and heavy. Everyone ran screaming and scampering, trying to find safety. Under my shirt, my ribs were bleeding. My organs felt crushed. I could barely breathe. I knew I needed to get up, but I couldn't. I closed my eyes.

My ribs throbbed so bad I thought I would die. "Get up!" Christopher yelled at me. I thought he would help me up, but he was so scared he tried to climb up a tree to the side of me. My vision was getting better. I had no time to complain. This was the buffalo's territory, and I wasn't intending to stay long.

I got on my hands and knees and tried to stop the ringing in my ears. Then I got to my feet. I stabilized myself. I limped over to the tree that Christopher was on. The tree wasn't the largest in the forest, but it was sturdy.

I grabbed a limb and pulled myself up. I grabbed another limb, to get myself higher up the tree. After I had climbed for a minute I stood up on a branch and rested. Next, the buffalo hit the tree, hard, with its horns. "Man, this buffalo sure has anger issues. We have to stop it," I exclaimed enthusiastically.

"I'm not going down there," Christopher yelled. I looked down at the massive buffalo. I still felt unexplainable pains in my gut. If we were going to move on, I had to stop the buffalo.

I jumped high into the air, towards the giant, black buffalo. I landed on its back. I landed, facing the rear end. I spun around and grabbed one of the horns. I punched the buffalo right behind the ear. The punch hurt my hand but seemed to do no damage to the buffalo.

The buffalo slammed its huge side against a tree. I trembled, but I held onto its horns and held my balance. I didn't know what to do.

I pulled the horns of the buffalo back. Then the buffalo jumped up. I lost my grip and flew into the air. I plummeted to the ground and skidded against the rocks and dirt. My knees were bloody with gashes. "That didn't work," I murmured. Everything hurt, but I had to keep moving

"Do something!" Chloe ordered.

I looked at her in disbelief. "What do you think I am doing," In a split second, I thought the buffalo might kill me. The buffalo was fast, and, suddenly it was right on me. I rolled to the side quickly, and the buffalo rammed into a tree. I stood up. I couldn't keep dodging the buffalo forever. I needed to end the fight.

Just as I had that thought, my legs began to shake in terror and pain. I felt as if my legs would collapse. Goosebumps popped up all across my body. My eyes welled with tears.

I fell to the ground, and everything went blurry. I thought I was about to die. I couldn't move, and the buffalo was coming back around. The world went silent and blurry. My body went limp. The last thing I saw as I blacked out, was the flash of something sharp and golden, flying towards the beast.

As I started to recover, a teenager I didn't recognize ran up with a large emerald rock and launched it at the buffalo's leg. The buffalo wobbled then fell to the ground. A very muscular much larger teenager walked towards the buffalo.

Everything was spinning. I sprawled out, trying to regain my senses, and for the first time thought I might survive. I had done the best I could, but my best was not enough. After a few minutes of staring up at the thick, brown, branches that covered most of the sky, I regained my vision. My whole body ached from the beating I had taken. I looked at my knees. It was bleeding and had scrapes and cuts running up and down my legs. Rocks and gravel were stuck into my other knee. I felt like my entire body was bruised or broken.

I looked over to the teenager that had saved us. He wore a short sleeve red Nike shirt that made his muscles stand out. He had on gray shorts with black Under Armour socks. He had brown hair and a stone face. He was cleaning a brass carving with a piece of bark.

I could see this golden trinket was like mine. This object was in the shape of a flame, with razor-sharp blades. I tried to speak, but all that came out of my mouth was a severe cough.

A girl spoke, "Get the cloth you made Cody. He's injured." The girl wore blue jeans and a pink Gap sweater. She had golden, straight hair, and looked very young.
"Got it, Stacy," a young man replied.

This boy looked about a year younger than me, and he was a good size, but not even slightly as muscular as the kid who had saved us. He wore a blue t-shirt with skin color shorts that stopped before his knees. He also wore long black socks and had a gray and a skin color mixed cloth. He took the cloth and wrapped it around my bloody knee.

He ripped off a piece and cleaned the rocks out of my other knee. I screamed in agony. The pain was excruciating. He wrapped my other knee after he had cleaned out the rocks. Stacy grabbed me by the legs, and he grabbed my shoulders. They drug me over to a log. My head now rested on a folded blanket against a log.

"You okay there?" the large teenager asked in a deep voice.

"I am okay," I responded raspily. I closed my eyes. I had been through the worst ordeal of my life today, and I still had to not become the liability of tomorrow. I soon fell asleep with the fear I might not survive this place.

Chapter Five

     I awoke the next day in a leather bed. Two poles were on each side of me, then leather strapped between them, like a hammock. I was in a grove, with giant hemlocks that appeared as if they were large enough to scrape the moon. I could smell blueberries. As I looked around, we were near a stream, and there were kids everywhere.

     I got out of bed and stood up. My whole body ached, but not as bad as yesterday. I could at least walk. I saw kids constructing a large tree house in between two closely spaced hemlocks. The girl that had told the boy to get the cloth yesterday was sitting near me. "You are up," she said in a soft soothing voice.

     "Yeah, I am just happy I am alive," I responded. She chuckled, and so did I.

     "I am Stacy. I am almost ten, and who are you

     I replied, "My name is George, George Grant, and I am thirteen. Nice to meet you, Stacy."

     "You too," she responded, "Do you want to come to meet the rest of us

"That would be great," I said. We walked over towards the group, where everyone was contently building and scavenging for supplies. In the forest, Stacy asked, "If you didn't come from the plane crash, then how did you get here.

I replied, trying to overlook the pain in my legs, "Well I don't really know."

"What do you mean she asked."

I responded, "I remember nothing really. I woke up from sleep, and I was on the sandy beaches of this island. I have no memory I'm obviously ok, but no memory at all."

"That is brutal but ironic," she stated.

"What do you mean by ironic, like why is it ironic," I asked.

She replied, "Ralph and Jack have that same story, and they didn't get here on a plane either." My brain spun. The thought of three teenagers that had the same unusual experience on the same island, was crazy.

We came up to a group, working on the treehouse. Stacy started by introducing the first teenager I had not met yet. "This is Cody," Stacy informed, while she pointed to the kid that had put the cloth around my knees yesterday.

He spoke, "It is nice to meet you, well at the least when you don't look dead."

We both chuckled, then he asked, "How are your knees? That was very severe."

I responded, "They ache a lot, but I can still walk."

"That's good," he added.

We both laughed, and then he stated, "I better get back to work, but it is nice to meet you."

"You too," I said as Cody went back to work.

Stacy led me through the forest to a kid with sagging gray shorts and a red Under Armour shirt. He wore a fake gold chain, and he had black socks. He said, "Yo, I'm Elijah. I'm fifteen, how old you, dawg."

I responded, "I am George Grant. I am thirteen I believe. It is nice to meet you, Elijah was it?"

"Yep, bye," he responded.
Stacy and I turned and walked back through the thick forest. The grass was silky smooth and lush. In fact, the entire forest was lush and green. Animals scampered through the forest, as we walked. Brown bushy-tailed squirrels crawled into their holes in the trunks of trees. The sun shone through the gaps between the hemlocks.

"He was a little weird, wasn't he," Stacy stated.

We walked across a flattened area and into a small section of the crashed plane. It smelled horrid. Gray leather seats lined the isles. Chip bags lay across the floor. The entire plane was a twisted mess Adults and children, lay, as they had died in the burning wreckage. Busted parts and luggage were strewn everywhere.

A teenager who looked about sixteen was sitting, holding an adult's hand. The adult was on the floor, and the young man was crying. The teenager was bulky. He wore a gray tank top and joggers that were rolled up to his knees. He wore long black socks. His eyes were brown, and his hair was brown.

"Oh hey," he spoke in a deep voice.

"You okay," I asked.

"Yeah, I was getting leather and I just, whatever."

"My name is George," I stated.

"I know. I had to carry you for miles. My name is Jason."

"Sorry. I hope I can help," I answered.

"I better get back to work," he responded as he stood back up.

"Okay," I responded as Stacy redirected me.

We walked until we saw a girl bawling off in a distance. She was on her knees. She wore an Old Navy gray shirt with denim blue jeans. "Her name is Isabella. She is seven, so this is a lot to take in for her. It is for all of us, but mostly for her," Stacy informed as a tear fell down her face. Her grin turned to a frown. "I am sorry. I wish there was something I could do," I spoke to her.

"It is okay," she mourned, "follow me," she said. We walked Now to the kid that had saved me the other day. He was more muscular and bigger than everyone else. His muscles bulged, and he was large in stature. I immediately praised, "Hey thanks for what you did yesterday. I was in over my head, and nothing I did seemed to phase it. You killed it so easily."

"Hey, it was a simple thing," he retorted.

"No, it was a big thing. You are amazing," I stated.

"Thanks," he responded.

"I heard you have had the same thing happen to you that happened to me." I blurted. He replied, "Wait you mean, you woke up on the island, and your brain is so jacked up, you can't remember your past."

"Yep," I stated, "And I saw something you threw at the buffalo. Do you have it on you?"

He spoke, "Yeah this thing just ended up in my pocket when I first got here. It works great as a throwing star." He held up a brass figurine. The carving appeared like a flame, and it was as sharp as a knife. "Wow!" I praised.

"It is cool, isn't it," he said.

I agreed, "Yep, but the real reason I am amused is because of this." I showed him my thin brass tree figurine with twisting branches.

"How?" he asked.

I responded, "I don't know. I know just as much as you do, and that isn't a lot."

He declared, "There must be something behind that, we must have something in our past."

"But what is it?" I asked.

"I don't think we will get that info here on this island," he conveyed.

"We have to find a way off this island," I stated.

Ralph declared as he put a hand on my shoulder, "Before we go with the bigshot ideas, let's start out with the little ones, like building a home."

"Hey what do you want me to do to help?" I asked.

He replied, "Oh, do not worry about it. I don't want your knee getting sprained or broke. We don't have medical treatment for that kind of stuff."

"Oh, don't worry," I said.

He stated, "No, seriously, we can't have you out there."

"Okay," I said, obediently.

Stacy showed me around. First Stacy walked me through the forest to a pond. The pond had clear fresh water. Lush green grass spread around the pond. The pond was deep and had a neat array of trees around it. I drank from the waters, and I took the cloth off my knees, then I put my legs into the water. I put the cloth around my knees, and we walked back towards where all the teenagers were working on making a tree-house in the hemlocks.

Stacy showed me the larger part of the plane, but she didn't go in with me. The plane was gray with two red stripes on each wing. The side of the plane appeared ripped out, and one wing had flown hundreds of feet away from where the plane lay. People lay miles away from the plane. The scene was gruesome. Inside was worse, with people everywhere, and the plane had crumpled like a tin can. It was a terrible scene and many of the kids were inside, working. I looked through the window and saw them ripping off the leather of the seats, for beds and materials. The kids were bawling, and they held their shirts to their nose, because of the smell.

Rivers ran across and through the jungle. After spending most of the day meeting people and looking at the beauteous jungle, I watched the sunset. My legs were still, very sore, because I had walked around most of the day, and the more I walked the more my knees ached. My legs shook as I sat down.

Later, Cody served a chicken he had caught and cooked over the fire. This was my first meal, and I was starving. As I bit into the amazing chicken, I said, "Thank you, Cody, for preparing this meal. This tastes great."

"Oh, no need to thank me," he responded.
Jack added, "No seriously, this is good."

Everyone responded with a cheerful look.

"Thanks," Cody replied. I gave Cody a fist bump and continued to eat.

"How are your knees?" Ralph asked.

I informed, "It hurts, and throbs terribly, after all the walking I did today, but I am much better than when I was at first."

Chris spoke, "That will take a while to heal."

I responded, "I know."

I spoke, "Hey, thanks for taking care of me, guys. You really did not have to do this, you don't even know me."

Christopher stated, "What are you talking about? You tried to kill a beast ten times the size of you, so we could be safe."

I added, "But I failed. Ralph saved you all."

Ralph said, "Except you tried, and that counts. You are brave."

"Thanks," I responded.

The night went on with a lot of laughing and funny stories. The kids were nice and had very interesting pasts. I sat back and listened. Soon, Jack yawned, and we went to bed. They helped me climb up a hemlock tree to a hammock. This hemlock was gargantuan. The tree had very smooth green leaves and a rough-barked trunk. I walked through the open doorway to seven beds. The beds were barely off of the ground, and they had leather filled with leaves. The beds were not the prettiest of beds, but they were good enough to sleep on. The home was simple but sturdy. On the second story were three beds, and a very long couch made of logs with leaf filled leather. I found a corner, laid down on a bed and fell asleep.

I awoke to a continuous tapping on the neck. "George, George," a voice whispered.

I moaned, "I am trying to sleep." A hand slapped my arm. I rolled over and got up. As I focused to clear my eyes. I saw it was Jack who had been tapping my arm. "Why did you have to wake me up?" I asked.

He held up a brass carving of a dolphin. "Because I figured something out about this," he responded pointing to his brass figurine.

"Do you have yours he asked. I showed my brass figurine. He asked, "May I see it?"

I responded. I gave him the brass figurine. He inspected this figurine, then stated, "Aha! Exactly as I thought."

"What is it I asked. Ralph walked over. Jack stated as he gave me my figurine back, "Inspect yours, then when you find a button press it."

"I found it," Ralph insisted.

I inspected until I found a button.

Jack ordered, "Press the button on my count, three, two, one!" I pressed the minuscule button, and the tree transformed in my hand. The tree was now a sphere with a round slot in the middle holding a small pearl. The pearl swirled with pure bright green colors moving and swishing around its smooth surface as if someone had filled it with magic.

"Wow!" I celebrated.

"Truly," Ralph responded.

"Yep," Jack said. I looked over, and saw Jack's was the same as mine except the colors were pure, sea blue, and clear. Ralph's was fire red, blue, and yellow. Ralph touched his pearl. "Whoa!" he hollered.

I asked, "What do you feel?"

"I feel power," he said. His eyes swirled red. I saw his muscles clenching, and his pearl died out in color.

I took a breath, then I touched my pearl. I immediately felt strength surging through my veins. Wisps of energy shot out through the air, then turned and shot back to me. I felt more powerful than anything I had ever felt before. My knees didn't hurt, and I felt like I could move a mountain. The pain I felt earlier disappeared, and I felt better than ever. It seemed as if every wisp of power that flew out in the air turned and moved back into our bodies. Soon, I felt all of my strength die, and all of us collapsed to the ground, unable to move.

Chapter Six

I had an unusual dream that night. I was dangling by the neck, from a yellow rope, tied to a large tree. I struggled to breathe. I was losing air the more I struggled. My strength was giving out. I was dying. I ordered, "Help me, please!"

"You feel the excruciating pain. The blood not getting to your head. The air you can't breathe. After this, I get to go home," Ralph spoke.

"You psychopath," I hollered. He chuckled.

The muscular teenager yelled, "Untie him!" Two teenagers came and untied me and brought me down right by where the water was about to fall. I was kneeling down, and the water soaked my clothes.

"This is what you deserve for what you did. I am surely not going to miss you."

"Why?" I asked.

"Huh, why," he chuckled. Ralph grabbed me. "No, no, no. Please? Don't do this." Ralph pushed me off the ledge into the air. I fell down at least a hundred feet, and the drop was at least a thousand feet. A dream had never felt this real. Air shot at my cheeks. My eyes hurt when I opened them. My hair flailed. Then as I hit the water, everything went black.

I was on the island on the sandy beach. The plants behind me were all burnt and dead. Everything in sight was gray. I had cuts and burns all across my body. I felt sluggish. The mountain was ablaze in a massive conflagration.

I turned around and saw the sea. The sea was different though. In a certain spot, it was blood red. I saw a body floating helplessly on the blood current. It was Jack. His entire body looked like it had been beaten and drug over rocks. "Jack! I hollered as he floated onto the beach. I darted to Jack, and I felt his head. Blood dripped onto my hand. Gashes were everywhere on his body. His clothes were burnt.

"What happened I asked.

"You failed us," he responded. Jack closed his eyes. His body was lifeless. I yelled, "*NO, JACK, NO!*"

I jumped up with fists out, then I realized I was awake and ok. I was breathing quickly, terrified by what had happened in my dream. I felt different. My knees didn't hurt. I was standing next to my bed. I saw my tree carving on the ground, so I bent over and grabbed it, and I placed it in my pocket. I felt more energy than ever.

I got up and walked over to the hole in the treehouse to get out. I jumped down and grabbed a branch. I slowly climbed down the treehouse. Voices boomed outside. The sky was dark and filled with clouds.

Everyone was out playing games. Some played kickball and others were throwing pine cones into a reed hoop. "You are up. I thought you were dead for how long you slept," Arthur stated.

"Where are Jack and Ralph?" I asked.

Stacy who was standing near Arthur responded, "I showed you the pond yesterday, right?"

"You did," I said.

She directed, "They are swimming in there with everyone else. They have been gone for quite a while."

"Cool," I thanked. I started off to where she had shown me the day before. As I walked, the plants seemed to grow greener ahead of me. I had never seen plants grow so quickly. The branches intertwined as they grew taller in front of me.

I was recalling what happened last night as I walked. I took my brass tree out of my pocket. I inspected the figurine until I found the button, I had pressed last night.

The tree transformed as it had last night into a sphere with a slot in it for the gem. My gem was different now though. It looked like a see-through ball with no color. It looked plain and different. I had so many questions, with no answers.

I heard screaming ahead, and I darted towards the pond. I was faster than I was when I first got to the island, which seemed odd, considering my injuries. Soon, I was there. Teenagers were shivering with goosebumps and hair standing on end. They all pointed to the pool. "What happened?" I asked.

Chloe answered while shaking, "Jack is, is, is in there with an alligator."

"Why doesn't he run?" I asked.

Chloe responded, "He thinks he can fight it."

I blurted, "That is ridiculous. He is an idiot to think that." Jack was not coming up, and I didn't know why.

"How long has he been down there?" I asked.

"Minutes," she replied. I needed to know what was going on. I took off my shirt, then I ran to the edge of the pond.

I jumped into the water. As I plunged into the water I was sucked up into a whirlpool. I spun in circles. I was swallowing water, and the water was shooting up like a fountain. I struggled for air, but the water controlled me. I was like jello with no control.

I tried to swim higher, but I was just being sucked in. There was an alligator by me. It was trying to bite my feet. A tooth scraped against my foot and drew blood.

I tucked my feet in, trying to avoid it. I would drown if I didn't get out. I was sucking in too much water. I soon closed my eyes. The pain was too much. The tornado of water was getting more powerful.

I shot off into the air and then plummeted to the ground. My shoulder hit the ground first, and I rolled until I hit a tree trunk with my head. The impact hurt, but not much. I sprawled out on the ground, then slowly got to my feet. Jack shot out of the tornado, with the alligator. Jack landed gracefully, and the alligator hit a tree. It lay on its back for a moment then flipped over and ran away into the forest.

"How?" I asked.

"Come with me George," Jack stated.

"Okay," I responded, and I followed.

As we walked through the forest I asked, "How did you do that?"

Jack responded, "I know this sounds crazy, but the water pushed me wherever I wanted to go. I wasn't swimming. The water pushed me, and that tornado of water, I just thought about it and the water did as I wished."

"What?" I inquired trying to fathom what he had just said.

He answered, "No joke. Don't you feel stronger? I do. I know it has something to do with last night. I can just feel it. We all felt the power as we felt the pearls. I think it gave me special abilities when I touched it." My jaw dropped. I tried to wrap my brain around this concept, but it was too crazy. I spoke, "I felt the power, but that is crazy talk. Superpowers."

He argued, "You have to believe me. I beat up a stinking alligator."

"I do," I responded.

"Has anything as unusual as that, happened to you?" he asked.

"No, I woke up," I responded, "Wait, there is something. I was running earlier faster than I have ever run before. I wasn't running at outrageous speeds or anything, it is just my knees." I unwrapped the cloth around my knees, and not one scar was on my legs.

"How?"

I responded, "I don't know."

"Something similar happened."

"What is it?"

He replied, "When I was off fighting the alligator it bit down on my shoulder, and now the wounds are gone."

I stated, "That is extraordinary."

"I can't believe I did that!" Jack blurted with excitement, "Think of all the things I could do. If I learn how to control my power better, I could do crazy things. This is so nuts!" I felt great for Jack, but I was jealous. I felt puny, but that sounded selfish.

"I am fine," I responded.

He spoke, "Okay, you look a little glum."

"No, I am fine," I stated.

He said, "I wish there were more danger and action, so I could try to activate my abilities again." Jacks face had a huge smile with huge bright eyes. I thought it was funny the way he looked at me, but it thrilled me that Jack was happy. At least one of us had found the bright side of having a million tragic events happen at the same time. At least what felt like a million tragic events.

"Do you hear that?" Jack asked.

I responded, "No, what is it?"

"Follow me," Jack ordered. He darted through the jungle, and I followed. Soon, I heard the noise. I saw flames engulfing the tree house and spreading across the trees. "Oh, not this again!"

I saw Ralph at the heart of the flames. As I looked closer and closer, I saw what was really going on. Ralph was doing the impossible. He was standing inches from the fire, and out of his hands came flames. He had a big grin on his face and continued to torch the jungle. "RALPH, STOP!" I hollered.

"I can't," he spoke. It petrified me. What if Jack were to die, and someone threw me off a waterfall hundreds of feet. It scared me. I was terrified but said nothing.

I saw a humongous column of water shooting through the air at an incredible speed. The water crashed, with a boom into the fire. Jack groaned. His face looked intense. He was controlling the water, but his power would not be enough. His face grew red. His skin became pale. Jack's eyes squinted. His back hunched. Saliva came out of his mouth. Jack's knees buckled.

Jack fell to the ground, and the water splashed to the ground. The fire did not stop. I knelt down. Jacks face was pale. He had no control over his body. His head felt very warm.

I shook Jack, but he did nothing. Tears streamed down my face. Jack looked lifeless. His face was pale. I tried everything in my power to get Jack to wake up, but nothing worked. Slapping only caused his face to jerk. Trying to do c.p.r on Jack did nothing, and only made me feel awkward. "Jack, please wake up. Please stop the fire," I pleaded.

Jack coughed up dirt. He was the only one that could save us. Suddenly, he moaned and awoke with a start. He stood up and immediately, then the water was blasting again. Jack managed to score a direct hit on Ralph, and he tumbled into the bushes. The fire died out and Jack passed out again.

I said, "Well on the bright side the tree house is still." The sound of the tree house interrupted me as it crashed to the ground. Everyone walked out of the bushes, from where they were hiding.

"Help Jack!" I hollered. They all ran over, and

I walked to Ralph. "Hey buddy," Ralph spoke.

I argued, "Are you retarded. How could you do such a thing?"

"Come with me," Ralph ordered

"Why did you keep on blasting?" I asked. Ralph swung his large fist at my face, it connected with my nose and I fell to the ground. Again, for the third time in 24 hours I was on the ground and bleeding. I almost blacked out.

Chapter Seven

Ralph and I walked through the jungle. "I saw a grin on your face when you were burning everything. Why?" I argued.

"Did you not see what I did. It was amazing. Jack got lucky to stop me. I am much stronger than he is. He passed out after just seconds."

"I saw you destroy everything of ours. Yeah, that was amazing. It was a show. I'll Do it again." I shook my head. We need to help each other survive, not demonstrate our power.

This made him angry and swung at me again. The blow glanced off this time, but it was enough to knock me to the ground again. My face hit the ground and bounced. I was bleeding from my mouth and something snapped in my mind.

I asked, "Hit me again. It feels great." Ralph came down with another striking blow to the face. I now had a goose egg on my chin. My mouth continued to bleed, and all of my teeth were covered in blood. Dirt flew into my eyes, and into my mouth. I felt as if I couldn't move my head at all.

"I was joking," I mumbled. Blood came out of my mouth as I coughed, trying to pick myself up. Ralph stated, "I had a visit from one of our brothers, last night. He was able to fly in at an incredible speed as if he were made of light. He landed in the room and transformed into his human form. He has special abilities also, but he is stronger than all of us. We are brothers, you, Jack, and I. He told me something interesting."

"**LIES!**" I mumbled as blood poured out of my mouth.

"I have proof," he argued. Ralph brought out a picture of a man with brown wavy hair, and an Adidas jacket. He looked around eighteen or so. He had gargantuan muscles, and Jack's sea-green and blue eyes. He was in the jungle with Ralph. "How?" I asked.

Ralph spoke, "He said you, Jack, and I all have special abilities. He said you and Jack blamed me for something I didn't do, and that got us all stuck on this island. He said you guys went against the cause of good. He also said he could get me off of this island if I kill you and Jack."

(Oh great, now I got a brother trying to murder me. Zippity dippity! Best day of my life).

"Even if I did those things before, which I did not, I'm not that person now." As I got on my feet, I had my fists up. My torn-up body was skinny, and could easily get knocked off balance. Ralph screamed at me "You are both against me and I will kill you first. He picked me up like I was a feather, then he kneed me in the head. I felt a pain that seemed to shatter my bones. Blood was gushing from my forehead onto my face. My vision went blurry, and every word that Ralph spoke was a blur. I lay helpless on the dirt.

A figure ran over. I recognized her. The person who had saved me many times. Her features differed from everyone else's. Her golden straight hair glistening in the sun. She grabbed my shoulders, and angrily drug me across the grass away from Ralph.

She set me up by the rest of the group. Some were sobbing, and some were angry and didn't know what to do. The safety we felt the night before was gone forever, and the future for all of us was unknown. They tried to help me. They gave me water and my strength slowly came back. I had less strength than I had walked into the conversation with, but I was somehow recovering faster.

Ralph left for a while but, then returned. Ralph pointed at us, "This kid, and Jack are the reason I am on this island. They lied about something I did not do, and that got me stuck on this island. I am sure they are the real reason your plane crashed."

Cody responded, "That is ridiculous. You made that up. Why didn't you tell us this before if that's what happened."

"I had a visit from my brother. He also has abilities. He can fly. He told me this," Ralph suggested.

Christopher then argued, "Jack and George would not harm a fly. They have done nothing wrong to us."

Ralph spoke, "That isn't true. George's has been hurt every step of the way, and you guys have had to pay for it. Think of it. Stacy, you've had to work the hardest here, because George is constantly getting hurt."

I hunched up. I put my hands on the ground and pushed myself up. My body hurt. My head felt nauseous as I stood up. My legs wobbled. I sauntered towards Ralph.

I looked up at Raph. He looked confident. I looked up at him, and I spoke my mind, "You better take a step back and look at yourself. You saved us once but ruined an entire day's work. You have almost burnt the entire jungle down, in a single day."

Ralph Looked down at me with no respect, and argued, "At least I can save everyone when they are in trouble. You couldn't even stop a buffalo. Imagine what I could do with my abilities."

Ralphs pointer finger lit a small flame. "You know what comes with helping me? I received a promise from my brother that if I kill them, I get to leave this island. If I kill them, I will free you guys. We should leave them here to rot and die as they deserve."

"*PSYCHOPATH!*" I hollered.

"Come with me, and I will spare your lives, but if you don't, you'll die as well. These kids can barely take care of themselves. I can take care of all of you," he stated. That infuriated me. He was much stronger than me, and it made me feel weak and powerless. He used this to his advantage.

A portion of the group walked over beside him, including, Marissa, Arthur, Chloe, and Elijah. Jason spoke, "Guys, you can't seriously believe him. This is a lie. How could you possibly ally yourself with him?"

Marissa answered, "Some things are too crazy to explain, but must be true."

"Come on! How?"

Arthur argued, "Jason, in life, there are two types of people. There are the survivors and there are the weak. The question is, which one are you?" Jason's eyes swelled. He walked towards Ralph.

"Good choice," Ralph spoke, "anyone else?" No one else followed him.

"Bye retards. Have fun rotting," Ralph said, as he walked away. I wanted to break all of Ralph's bones. Ralph pushed me, and I fell back to the ground. Something snapped in me again. My anger exploded.

Before I could get up, something shot past me. I felt a swirl of wind like something hit me. As I focused on what it was, I saw clearer. A root shot out of the ground and grabbed Ralph. It wrapped around his wrist and appeared to slowly swallow his arm. The branch strangled his arm, as his face poured sweat.

Ralph was furious, as he began to focus, intently, on the wood wrapped around his arm. The wood shriveled slowly. Fire shot out across his arm and soon burnt the entire branch. I sat up, and I restrained myself from trying anything else. Cody asked, "How?"

As I thought about the millions of how's in my life, I responded, "I don't know." Ralph dusted off his arm and walked off into the forest with the others. The rest of us mourned as we thought about the loss of our friends. I had made an enemy, and this would not be our only battle.

Chapter Eight

Everyone looked distraught, including me. This morning had been chaotic, and now we had a lot of work to do. There were fewer of us, and some of us were injured. Jack appeared badly hurt, and the rest of us were too upset to get up. Not only was I upset, but I was furious. My mind raced. I was even a little jealous of Jack and Ralph's abilities. I felt useless.

After a while, we decided it was time to get going.

"Time to get to work," I stated.

Cody replied, "Yeah, we probably should," as he took his hands off his forehead.

Isabella asked, "Same as last time," as she started to cry.

"Yep," I responded. We all walked off to look for supplies. We built higher on another hemlock. We hid the building, so it would be difficult for Ralph to find us. The large head on the trees shadowed the tree house. I picked up a large log. These logs were awkward to carry, so two people had to handle them. Climbing the tree was the most difficult part of the task.

Cody and I started working together. We started off searching around trees to find logs or broad branches. Soon, we would find a large enough branch and picked it up by both ends. We started to talk as we worked, to pass the time.

As we carried the branches, Cody asked, "What are we going to do with Ralph?"

I responded, "Yeah I don't know, he is so powerful and mean. We are going to have to protect the group."

Cody spoke, "You are tough. You end up on an island with amnesia, your own brother beats you to the pulp, and you have someone out to murder you. Must be fun." I laughed.

Cody asked, "What are you going to do when he comes?"

I responded, "Honestly, I do not know. We have Jack."

He responded, "True, but we probably need to have a game plan in case."

I spoke, "That's true. We probably should. Where do you think they are right now?"

Cody said, "I don't know. Maybe heading towards the water." We had now gone through a few logs, and we continued to talk as we worked. We moved a lot of logs together as everyone else did their part. We laughed and talked. Cody was easy to talk to and very funny. Soon, the bottom floor was constructed, and we took a break.

I walked over to the clean, clear watered river, to get a drink. I also took the time to wash my clothes in the river. After that I needed to dry the clothes, so I climbed to the top of a tall, full-grown hemlock, and hung my clothes up. While I waited, I skipped rocks across the pond. There were a lot of round and flat rocks around the pond. The water was calm, and there was no one around. The more I practiced, the better I got at skipping rocks. It was very relaxing, not to have to think for a few minutes. My clothes finally dried and I got dressed and walked back towards the hemlock where we were working.

Cody said, "It is hard to build it isn't it."

"Yep, it is. It's easier to just think of a design. Building it is much harder," I spoke.

"True," Cody said.

"I wish the tree house could build itself. I imagine beds with nice swirly carvings. Smooth walls. Modern beds. A top story, with two couches and a bookcase. Three beds on the bottom, and two on the top. A nice built-in ladder."

"Yep, that would be nice, wouldn't it," Cody stated as he gazed at what we had built our home.

"We probably should," agreed Cody. We went out into the jungle searching for any logs that would work. Truthfully, finding the logs was one of the hardest parts of this experience.

We saw a log that was large enough. The log was round and dark brown. Cody picked up the log on one side, and I picked it up in the other. We hauled it off towards the hemlock. I grunted and groaned as we walked back with the log. I thought, (We are going to be at this for weeks.) We got close to the tree house and as Cody looked up, he dropped the log. The log broke my grip and smashed down on my foot. "Oww! I blurted. Cody paid no **attention**.

"What is it?" I asked

Cody pointed at the hemlock, "That is why," he said as he stared in awe. I looked up at the tree house.

"It's done somehow," he stammered. It was as if we had been in the jungle for hours, but we were gone for minutes. Something had finished the construction and it was beautiful and large.

"Race you up there!" Cody yelled as he darted off towards the tree house.

I responded, "Oh like you will beat me," as I rocketed off towards the lengthy and lush hemlock.

I climbed up the branches, jumping from branch to branch. Cody was ahead of me. Cody kicked the branches off the tree, and they fell down. I dodged and tried to climb from branch to branch as quickly as I could. I coughed as dirt flew into my mouth.

Cody kicked my face occasionally. I was panting loudly, and was getting tired, but I continued to climb. My muscles clenched as I jumped from branch to branch. Soon, I was on the same branch as Cody, but it was too late. Cody was already jumping through the doorway. I climbed in after him. "Good job, second place."

"Funny," I said.

"This place is amazing!"

"It really is," I said. Three beds were on the bottom floor. They were all aligned, and a king-sized chair with armrests possessed many articulate designs. The beds included ornate carvings. This was exactly as I imagined the tree house when I wished it could build itself. We were the only ones in the tree house. A ladder was on the right wall. The ladder attached to the wall. Cody climbed up the ladder, and I followed.

Cody asked, "How did this happen. You imagined all of this perfectly."

"It is impossible," I stated. A nice bookshelf was close on the left wall. It was unique with the same swirling designs as the beds, and ladder, and the chair. Four shelves were in the bookcase. Two beds were exactly the same as the beds on the bottom floor. A king-sized couch was in the room, giant, long and perfect.

"This is unbelievable. Where did this come from?" Cody asked.

"This's indescribable," I responded. I was in awe. Cody spoke, "This is exactly as you explained it. Every single thing you had on your list is in here."

"What does this mean?" I asked.

"I don't know," responded Cody. I heard awes as more teenagers entered the tree house. Chris climbed up.

"How did this happen?" Chris asked.

Cody responded, "We don't know."

"What do you mean?" Chris inquired.

Cody spoke, "Well George said he wished the tree house could build itself, and he listed everything in this tree house. Then we walked over, and we saw it was complete."

"Impossible!" Chris marveled. Cody told the story to everyone, and we sat back and chilled. I sat down on the couch, and I rested. My worries left, and soon we all were hungry.

Cody said, "How about Christopher and I hunt, and George you build the fire pit, and Chris you kindle the fire."

"Sounds great," I responded.

Stacy asked, "What about us?"

Christopher responded, "No problem. We got this. Just sit back and chill." My stomach grumbled. I hadn't eaten all day. I had tried to drink water to replace the food, but that still wasn't enough. We had quail the night before, and that was probably the best meal I had on the island. I was ready to eat.

We all climbed down the tree. I rolled over the leftover logs that were not used for the tree house. I set these around the fire pit, and I dug a hole with a long stick. It wasn't deep, but it would work to hold a fire and keep us warm.

We put together a large pile of wood and Chris started it. I sat down and took out my brass figurine. This figurine had brought spectacular things. From the moment we had touched the pearls, everything changed. My life was out of control, but interesting. I wanted to look at my pearl color, to see if it had changed. I pushed the button on my tree.

It transformed but looked different than normal. It transformed into something much larger, and its color changed. It was a shield now. The color of the shield was silvery gray. There was a dark orange stripe towards the center. This material felt impenetrable, light, and easy to throw. The shield felt light but awkward in my hands. The shield had a firm handle. My jaw dropped.

"What just happened?" Chris asked.

I responded, "I told you about the night, right?"

"Yeah," he responded.

I informed, "Well it usually transforms into a spherical ball with a slot for my, now colorless gem. I must have clicked a different button. I have never seen it do this."

"May I hold it?" Chris asked.

I responded, "Sure thing." I passed over the gray, smooth, fine, shield. "It is light, but feels strong," Chris said.

"That is what I thought," I blurted.

"Mind if I try it out?" he asked.

"On what?" I asked.

He responded, "A tree, duh." Chris grabbed the handle and walked over to a tree about fifteen feet tall, and not that thick. He cocked back his arm, then he slammed the shield at a tree. There was a cracking noise, then the tree fell, altogether. "Whoa!" I celebrated.

"What in the world!" Chris stammered. I was astonished. "Thanks," Chris said. He handed it back to me, and I saw Cody walking over. I pressed the button in the middle of the shield. It transformed into its original size, form, and color. I placed it in my pocket. Chris was in shock. He had forgotten to find sticks for the fire. He darted off to find sticks and dead grass. I chuckled. Cody was walking over with the backpack. Cody asked, "Where is Chris?"

I responded, "Well you know Chris. Goofs off too much, then forgets to do his task, so he has to do it the last minute."

Cody laughed. "Where's the food?" I asked.

"In the pack," replied Christopher.

"What is it?" I inquired.

Cody replied, "Apples, lettuce and grapes. It is light, but there's a lot of it."

"Do you want to get the girls, Christopher?" I requested.

"Sure, no problem," he responded.

Cody spoke, "You know what I realized?"

"No, what?" I responded.

Cody stated, "We forgot about Jack. When I said we should get food and fire, Jack was not in the same room."

"Yeah what," I responded with a chuckle.

I said, "So I showed you my tree carving, right, and told you about that night?"

"Yeah!" Cody stated.

"Well, watch this," I said. I took out my tree carving. I pressed the button with glee. The carving transformed into the gray color as it did before. It was light but strong. It had the same smooth texture. It was amazing to hold and felt supernatural, as if it had a hidden source of power. Cody's jaw dropped. He stammered, "How, what, how did you do that?"

I smiled as I answered, "I honestly was searching for the button to turn this thing into an orb earlier, and I pressed another button on accident, and this happened."

"Fascinating!" he responded, "Mind if I hold it. It is fascinating."

"That is exactly what Chris asked. Sure," I said. I passed the shield over, so he could hold it. Cody examined the shield. "It is lightweight, but it feels strong and powerful."

"That is what I thought," I said.

"It's cool, isn't it?" Chris exclaimed as he walked over. Chris went to work as he kindled the fire. "It should be a great tool to help us," I stated.

Cody passed me the shield, and I turned it back into its tree form. I placed it in my pocket. Christopher walked over with the girls and Jack. Jack had red lines under his eyes. His head drooped. I knew he felt exhausted.

"How was your sleep?" I asked Jack.

"What?" he responded while scratching his head. I laughed. Cody handed out curved sections of wood. "Where did you find these?" I asked.

"We ripped the outside, bark shell off a young tree so it was smooth," he responded.

Cody and Christopher dispersed the salad out equally on the makeshift plates. I ate with my hands. The apples and grapes added a great texture to the salad. The salad tasted crunchy and light. Even with this food, I was still very hungry. The fire was cozy and felt great with the chill wind. After I finished, I spoke, "Thank you, guys."

"You helped too," Cody said. After sitting and talking for a while, we went up to the tree house. It was a long day and we had accomplished a lot. I climbed up the limbs of the tree. I was so tired, my eyes continued to close, while I was climbing.

Soon, I grabbed a bed on the top floor. I lay leather across my bed that the others had ripped off the seats of the plane. The beds had been stocked with leaves inside the leather, and it made a great cushion. Cody sat on the bed to my left, and Christopher to my right. I closed my eyes, content with the day and glad to be with a good group of friends. Sleep came quickly....

Chapter Nine

A few days passed of normal work and play. The days were not easy, hunting, hauling water, and building, but we knew what we were doing. For a bunch of kids, there was a lot of work and responsibility. Food was the biggest challenge. Days of hard work were frustrating, but sometimes, things were good. I wondered where Ralph was. Most of the mysteries that happened here, we had to leave alone, because there were no answers. Days passed with no visits from Ralph or any miraculous events. I helped with work, then we would go swim, and eat at day's end, and that was the best part of the day. We told funny stories, jokes, and had a great time. Everyone seemed to get along. We sat back and relaxed and enjoyed the downtime we had. We didn't worry about Ralph. I hoped he had gone to the other side of the island. That was a mistake.

....

I was half asleep in the night when I heard creaking. The sound of footsteps on the floor below me. I was tired, mostly asleep, so I ignored what I heard. Soon, the creaking stopped as I heard something climbing down the tree house. I fell back asleep carelessly.

I woke up very early, but I couldn't go back to sleep. I climbed down the stairs, so I could go get water from the pond. As I climbed down the ladder, I saw footprints on the ground. Mud tracks from at least two people, and what looked like something being dragged behind them. I remembered the creaking during the night. I climbed up the ladder to my room. I walked over by Cody's bed, and I tapped his arm.

"What?" asked Cody with his eyes still closed.

"Get up now. Someone took Jack," I said.

"I know someone, or something took him," I said, but Cody was already asleep.

I grabbed Cody's arm again, and added, "Ralph was here. He took Jack and might be coming back!" Cody jumped out of bed.

"Where is he?" he asked.

"I don't know, but I am convinced Ralph took

jack," I responded. Cody followed me downstairs.

I whispered, "See how there are three muddy footprints, and last night it rained. Jack is the only one gone."

"Oh, gosh!" Cody whispered.

"We have to go get him," I said.

I informed, "If we go by ourselves, I think we can rescue Jack. Jack is the most powerful person here. We need him. We can't risk everyone's lives. I think you and I can find the camp and rescue him."

Cody thought, then committed, "Okay." We grabbed some supplies, then went back down the treehouse. We found the tracks on the ground and followed them.

As we traveled farther into the jungle, it was interesting. New sights and sceneries made everything beautiful. Mud stuck to our shoes. Marshes stretched out so far, we had no choice but to walk through them. Everything was green and lush.

The tracks headed in the direction of the mountain and seemed endless. Jack could not have wandered this far. There must have been something or someone that took him. It was frightening to consider, but something about the jungle put me at ease.

It was strange to be in this situation, stuck in the jungle, trying to survive with people trying to kill us. At the same time, we were on this beautiful island with the most gorgeous scenery I had ever seen. Being somewhere that was so beautiful, almost balanced out the fear.

My thoughts turned back to Jack. He was not a guy to wander off. There were three tracks, and only one person was missing. We had been walking for a solid three hours. I was scared of getting lost myself. Ralph was out to kill me somewhere on the island. There were animals all over the island, like the buffalo. Whatever had taken Jack, was overpowering him, and I was not as powerful as Jack. "What is the game plan?" Cody would ask.

"I don't know," I would say every time. I had no plan, and every time I came up with one, I would throw it out as too risky. I was jittery and unsure. I believed I was smarter than Ralph, but with his powers, I could see no advantage over him. I didn't understand what had happened with the tree house and Ralph's arm. He had abilities like no other, and Jack had those same abilities, and that is why I needed him. As we got closer to the mountain, Cody worried, "This is a bad idea. Maybe we should go back and get the others."

"And leave Jack to die," I responded. Ralph was very intimidating, as I considered having to fight him. I was sweating, and my legs and arms were trembling at the thought of what was to come.

Soon, I saw gargantuan marks. They almost looked like snake marks, but they were the size of boulders. I heard a deep hissing. Then, something knocked us both off our feet. I spun high in the air. The thing that had hit us was enormous. I flailed, as I plummeted down to the ground. I landed, face first in the dirt. I swallowed dust, and my elbow hurt from the impact as did my nose. I swallowed some mud.

"What was that?" Cody asked.

"Shh," I whispered. I ran behind a tree, and Cody followed. "What do we do?" Cody asked. I transformed my shield ready for combat. "You think you can save us with that?" he asked.

"Hopefully," I whispered back, "Stay here." I looked around the tree. I saw what the beast was. It was impossible. I couldn't believe my eyes. Those marks were snake marks. The snake was orange and black, covered in thick, armor-like scales. The snake was at least fifteen feet wide, and probably hundreds of feet long. The sight made me pause for a moment. I exclaimed, "Yeah, that will take more than a shield."

"What is it?" Cody whispered.

"I can't explain," I responded. Soon, the snake was staring right at me with it's tongue out. Tears welled in my eyes. My face went red and sweat poured down my face.

I was scared out of my mind. My breathing was heavy. My mind was racing.

"RUN!" I hollered. Cody and I bolted. The snake slithered after us. We raced towards a tree, and we climbed. "We're gonna die!" Cody screamed.

"Maybe," I responded. We climbed as fast as we could. The tree broke as the snake slithered farther up. "George?" Cody questioned.

"I know, just stay calm," I responded. The tree continued to crack. I was becoming more frightened. The snake was getting closer, and a fall from this height could be fatal. The snake could easily rip us to shreds. I was losing options as if I had any to start with. The tree was large but couldn't bear the load of this beast. The snake was fast and moving up quickly, as It hissed at us. "***WHAT DID WE EVER DO TO YOU***?" Cody bawled.

I threw my shield down at the snake. The shield shot down at the snake but bounced off of the snake's impenetrable scales. "What did I do to piss you off?" I hollered at the snake.

The snake suddenly turned and slithered down the tree. "Good, the shield must have worked," I celebrated. As I spoke this, I felt the tree shake. We could feel the tree was about to fall. We started climbing down as fast as we could, without falling. As we climbed, we heard cracking and snapping all around us.

We reached the ground, just as the tree collapsed. The tree fell, kicking up dirt and rocks high into the air. The snake stared at me, and it looked hungry. Snakes by themselves frightened me, but a two hundred-foot long snake petrified me. I was panting and didn't know what to do. I couldn't outrun this beast, and I had to protect Cody.

The snake slithered as fast as it could. I stood still, frozen in shock. The snake smashed its head against me. The impact was tremendous. I felt like I would explode. It sent me flying, high into the air.

I hit my back against a tree and slid down in a lump. Blood ran down my back. I felt the scrapes and pieces of bark, sticking into me. I had never felt so much pain, but I knew if I didn't get up, we were both dead.

"RAAGH!" I hollered in a rage. Again, something snapped, and I felt energy surging through me. Power with endless possibilities mixed in my mind. A strength I never felt before whirled through my veins. I grabbed my fallen shield!

The snake slithered at me simultaneously, ready to strike. Its tongue hissing, and its orange eyes staring me down. It flashed its scales. I had no fear now. I felt invincible.

Suddenly, I understood what my power was. Jack possessed a carving of a dolphin, and his pearl was made of blue energy. Jack controls the sea. Ralph has a carving of fire, and he controls fire. The plants grew days before, as I walked past them. I had a tree carving. I could control plants.

The snake lunged at me with ferocity. I put my hand in the air, calling for my power to show itself. I tried to control a tree near me.

My strength surged. The tree shook, but no more than that. I called upon the roots to snap. They did, and the tree pulled free into the air. I shot the tree at the snake.

It spun ferociously, as I guided it straight at the mouth of the snake. It opened its mouth as if to bite it but, the tree crashed through its fangs and into the deepest part of its mouth. I made sure the trunk shot far into the snake. It was surely dead.

The beast's head plummeted to the earth. Rocks and dirt shot up. Venom spilled from its fangs, onto the ground.

The energy I felt, left me. The power surging through me, slowed. "What just happened?" Cody asked.

I responded, "I think I know what the abilities I possess are."

He stepped out from behind the tree where he was hiding.

Cody asked, "What are they?"

I spoke, "Well, it explains what happened a few days ago. The day when the tree house formed, I wished that the tree house could make itself, and it did. That same day when I walked towards the pond, the plants grew around me as I walked. When Ralph tried to leave, a branch wrapped around his arm. All these events happened because of me. I can control plants. I can't really control them perfectly, yet, but that is definitely my ability."

Cody said, "Well that is great. Now we have a way to fight Ralph and get Jack back. We have two people on our side with abilities. He will be on his own against the two of us." I knew what I could do now. If felt powerful. My confidence grew. I was ready to fight.

I heard a sound like a boomerang, and something smashed against the back of my head. "George!" Cody yelled as I passed out, falling to the ground.

Chapter Ten

I opened my eyes, to a black world, that I didn't know. Rock stalactites hung, down from the ceiling. I was slumped on a cold black stone. The air was cool and frosty. A small light from somewhere in the distance, shone in, through the darkness. "Oh, he is awake," a voice I recognized said.

He spoke, "Hello, how's it going?"

I responded, "Oh great. Kidnapped by a psychopath and his morons, so I'm doing great."

Arthur shot back, "You are lucky you're still alive. Ralph is being very generous." I tried to think of the ways he was being generous, nothing came to mind.

I retorted, "Ralph is being nice? He knocked me out, put me in bonds, even kidnapped my friend, and is now trying to kill me. He is so generous."

"You better watch what you say. Everything you say, I'll report."

"You keep him here while I get him," I heard from a voice nearby.

"Why are you following a psychopath?" I asked.

Arthur explained, "I went with the Alpha on the island. You can't keep us safe, and he can bring us home if he kills you. I want to go home."

I asked, "Then what. Where will you go? Your family is dead. How will anyone know where you are? He's lying to you." Arthur mumbled and stopped talking. I heard voices getting closer. I wanted to break my bonds and run.

I was too weak to move, let alone break my bonds. My head throbbed from being hit in the back of the head. I was nauseous. I heard a deep voice, echoing off the walls of the cavern. Ralph was here. I wanted to move, to fight, but I couldn't.

"You're up," I heard the deep voice of Ralph.

"Where is Jack?" I immediately asked.

He responded, "Don't worry. He is safe, for now."

I shrieked, "If you lay a hand on Jack, you don't even know what I will do to you!"

Ralph laughed, "I like your enthusiasm."

"Where am I?" I asked.

Ralph answered, "In a cave below the mountain."

Ralph spoke in his evil deep voice, "I have had many more visits from our brother. He is stronger than both of us. He has an amazing cause. I want to help it, but I can't do that with you still alive."

"You are a psychopath!" I hollered.

"Is that what you think?" he responded. My fists clenched. His smugness infuriated me.

"Where is Cody?" I asked.

"I've taken care of him. I have no problem with him. He's a nice kid." I looked at Ralph with pure rage. His eyes sparkled in the dark cave. "Bring him to the falls," Ralph ordered.

Two teenagers picked me up and dragged me out of the cave. I was dragged through the grass and at least a mile up the mountain. It was again a contradiction. Here I was being drug to my death, though some of the most beautiful landscapes in the world. We arrived at the top of the mountain, which was made of black granite, with white speckles.

A large pond that led into a waterfall was at the top. A quaint shack, that looked about two rooms long, sat to the side, by a maple tree. They cuffed my hands and legs with leather, and I was being helplessly dragged.

"Hang him," Ralph ordered.

"Yes," Ralph responded, "And Jason help."

Jason spoke, "No disrespect, but I don't think I can kill someone."

Ralph ordered, "Do you want to leave this island alive?"

"Yes," Jason gulped.

"Then do it or else," Ralph stated.

I was being hoisted up a beautiful maple tree, with unique orange leaves. They stopped halfway up the large trunk and strapped my neck to the tree. My arms and legs were still tied, and I was in a panic. I had no ability to fight what was happening. I saw Cody walking out of the shack. "George!" he yelled. His eyes were red and swollen.

Suddenly, something out in front of me made my heart sink and my blood boil. Jack was tied up in a heap and was laying in the water. They picked him up and knelt him down right on the edge of the waterfall. He looked as if he were already dead, and as if it was pointless to fight back. "Jack!" I hoarsely yelled, but only a whisper came out. I was struggling to breathe, and my neck was throbbing. Part of me wanted to just let go and stop fighting and disappear into the blackness. My mind came back to me, as my rage started to build.

I saw Ralph by Jack. "See everyone. This happens to jerks like Jack and George. As I said, there are two types of people in this world. There are survivors, and there are the weak. Jack has chosen his side, and that is why he's about to die."

Ralph grabbed Jack's shoulders and whispered something into his ear. I struggled to stay conscious and focus on what was happening I wasn't going to last much longer. I had to find a way to break free. Ralph hollered, "Jack will witness a heartbreaking fall, literally."

"No!" I spoke, but no one could hear. I looked around for something, anything I could do. I tried to think of something to get us out of this nightmare. I struggled for breath and felt myself dying. Jack would follow me, soon. I needed to act. There were too many of us that need protection from Ralph. I still searched, frantically looking for a solution. Jack would die, and it would be my fault. The wind shook the tree. *Pinecone*, I thought.

I focused on a large pine tree on the other side of the river. There had to be one there. Then, I saw it. *Pinecone*. I needed to use my power. "Ralph, please don't do this," Jack pleaded.

"Why not? I have everything to gain," Ralph responded.

"You can't. This is too terrible, even for you," Jack spoke.

Ralph responded, "I did not get to know you that well. I think I will be fine."

I felt a rush of adrenaline. I felt dizzy. I could barely see. I reached my tied hands out in the direction of the pinecone, far off and below me on the mountain. The pinecone sat still, nothing happened. "No," I spoke.

The pinecone wobbled then jumped. It jumped, but nothing more. I could feel the power build, as I struggled for air. The pinecone was out of my reach, and I could barely get it to move. I focused on the anger, and the pinecone levitated, but I couldn't get it to move towards me. It was so easy when I wasn't trying. Why was it so hard now when I needed it? I could move things so well when I was frightened or infuriated. I looked back towards Jack.

Ralph spoke, "You know, murder is a horrible and final thing. You'd think I would feel sorrow or shame, but I feel fine."

"Please Ralph. I am your brother. You said so," Jack pleaded.

Ralph argued, "Who cares. Cousin, brother, friend, enemy. If they do something to you that is cruel, and you will get rewarded to do something cruel back, you can do anything you want."

"You have no heart," Jack stuttered. My neck was about to break. The pinecone still levitated, nothing more. I was slowly starting to black out again. Ralph stated, "Once I kill you, Jack. I will have murdered the strongest person other than me, on the island. Killing everyone else will be easy."

"George will save them," Jack spoke.

Ralph argued, "Well George is back there, hanging from his neck, so it's over." Jack slumped over in defeat. "Don't worry," Ralph said, "You won't feel this pain for much longer."

"The sun will shine on you again, George," Jack yelled.

"You are just like George," Ralph exclaimed.

"Have fun on the way down," Ralph said as he pushed Jack off the edge.

"*NO*!" I hollered. My anger spiked. I felt the energy start to build from my rage. I couldn't save Jack and now he was dead. My heart pumped, and I felt strength growing. The same energy I had felt before. I was ready to fight. I reached my arm towards the pinecone.

The pinecone transformed into a long, sharp, wooden knife, and shot through the air so fast, I almost couldn't see it. It transformed and shot towards me, as soon as I had the thought. The wooden knife came at me. It cut the leather strap around me, with precision, and I fell to the ground. I ripped the bonds from my hands, and feet. "**JACK!**" I screamed, "**RALPH, YOU MURDERER!**" I slammed my fist against the granite rock. Ralph saw I was free and laughed, "You could've saved him, but you didn't."

I screamed, "You killed him."

He responded, "You didn't stop me!" I levitated the wooden knife into the air. It floated by my right side.

"Oh, you've discovered one of your powers," he spoke.

"One of them?" I asked.

"You will die for what you did," I raged. Power surged in me. Energy flowed through my body. I felt strong enough to take on anything. I glared at Ralph. He had to be stopped.

My mind went to work. Suddenly, a thousand needles pierced the air, flying past me at incredible speeds. They shot towards Ralph. They were blackberry thorns. I had seen them as they drug me up the mountain. They hit Ralph so hard, it knocked him off his feet. There were so many, he was almost covered in them. He screamed in pain. Blood poured from his body. I saw fear in his eyes, as he fell to his knees.

Suddenly, his whole body was engulfed in flames. I had never seen Ralph do this before. The flames made him look much larger than normal. He looked powerful and ominous.

Ralph exclaimed, "YOU THINK YOUR POWER COMPARES TO MINE."

"Turn back," I yelled

Ralph unexpectedly changed back to his normal form, as if that had drained too much power. His appearance looked less powerful.

Ralph offered, "You know. Whoever sent us to this island knew about our power because these clothes don't burn." I walked towards Ralph, still raging with power. I ordered, "You need to stop this."

Ralph swung at me. He punched me in the jaw with great force. Again, my mouth throbbed, and I fell to the ground. My head spun, but only for a minute. Blood built up in my mouth. I spat it out.

I had a split second to act, while he was walking towards me. I saw a pinecone off in the distance. I closed my eyes. I concentrated. I felt the life and the organism of the plant. The pinecone shook, then levitated. It shot towards us. Ralph swung at me. I put my hand in his direction, still laying on the ground.

I felt the air swish past my head and braced for the impact. Slowly I looked up and saw exactly what I had imagined. Ralph was inside a tree. His arm was sticking out. The tree had twisting branches, and a large trunk, and was tall as a skyscraper. The tree was colossal and dark brown I heard mumbling, but it was not clear, because it came from inside the tree.

"How're you doing in there?" I asked.
I knocked on the wood. There was no answer.

"Great, nice chat."

I knew that would not restrain him for long. I got up. I was shaking. Everyone else stood, staring me.

I thought, and branches reached out and wrapped around all of them, locking them to the tree. I darted towards the lodge. I stood in the doorway.

"Cody?" I said, checking to see if he was there.

"George," he responded. I heard the crackling of the tree, and I saw flames bursting out of the thick trunk. He would be out soon. "We need to go," I offered. Cody ran to the doorway. "You beat him," he spoke in amazement.

"Yeah," I responded.

"Thanks," he said. I heard more crackling.

"We need to go," I said urgently

"Let's go," he responded, "Wait, what about Jack."

I didn't answer

He paused, "Ohh gosh!"

"He pushed him over the edge," I said. Cody immediately started to sob. Then, I heard Ralph yell, "George!"

I urged Cody, "We really need to go." He responded, "Okay." We darted out, down the mountain, and into the rainforest. We traveled the same route the same way we had come. This time, one less person than we had hoped, when the day started.

Chapter Eleven

The walk back was frustrating. "What are we going to tell them.?" Cody asked. I got lost in my thoughts, but I was too upset to focus. I couldn't believe what had happened. "I can't believe Jack is dead. I am sorry," Cody said.

I responded, "I kind of felt like he was the only person I had. He was my brother, and I felt like that was my only connection to whatever home I had."

"Sorry," he comforted. We walked through the forest, trying to figure out what to do now. I couldn't even describe what had happened. I was so sad; my head was all over the place. I sobbed at the thought of Jack being gone. Nothing was going to be easy going forward, and we still had to tell the group about Jack.

I could feel anger beginning to boil again. I'm sure I had the power to stop Ralph, and to stop Jack's death, but I had done none of those things. Ralph was still out there, and Jack was dead. Ralph was probably right. I probably lied and got him stuck on this island. I had no answers and I felt as though I had done something wrong.

Cody tried to cheer me up with, "It wasn't your fault. It was Ralph's," but nothing could cheer me up at this point

As I looked towards the treehouse, I said, "I can't go up there. I can't."

"They have to know," Cody spoke.

"They will hate me."

"They will hate me also," he responded.

"You're right. They deserve to know what happened."

Cody spoke, "Well then. Let's go." As I walked towards the tree, I felt as if I were doing the right thing. I climbed up to the treehouse, limb by limb. As I entered the doorway, I saw all of their faces in distress. As they saw Cody and I, they jumped up and Stacy asked, "Where were you guys?"

I spoke, "Jack was taken during the night, and we followed Ralph through the rainforest to try to save him."

Christopher Responded, "Are you crazy? What happened?"

Chris asked, "Where is Jack?"

Cody stuttered, "Oh, um, he uh…."

"He was killed," I blurted.

"How?" Stacy asked as everyone started to sob.

I responded, "Ralph knocked us out and tied us up. He hung me by my neck from a tree, and they beat Jack and hauled him to the edge of a giant waterfall. I couldn't get free in time to save him. He threw him off."

Isabella asked, "How did you escape?"

Cody spoke, "George used his power and broke the bonds, then he beat…."

Chris interrupted Cody, and said, "If you could break the bonds. Why couldn't you save him?"

Cody spoke for me, "He did his best. He fought off Ralph enough to get us out of there."

Isabella cried, "Your best was not enough. Jack is dead." She sobbed.

Stacy patted Isabella's back as she spoke, "It is okay. You will be okay."

"I tried guys. I am sorry," I spoke.

Christopher spoke, "You tried your best? Your best was not enough and now Jack is dead."

"Guys," Cody said.

Chris argued, "Where were you when Jack fell?"

"I was inside Ralph's house," he responded.

"Were you in bonds?" asked Chris.

Cody responded, "No."

"You could've saved him," Chris blurted.

"I don't have powers," he responded.

"Neither does George," Chris stated.

I was about to leave, but that would have only hurt their feelings more.

Chris asked, "Why didn't you get us to help you. We could have saved him."

"I didn't want you to get hurt," I responded.

He revolted, "What, do you think you are stronger than the rest of us?"

"I have powers," I responded.

"Lies," Stacy stated. They hollered at us for what we had done. Cody and I left the tree house. They were angry and were only going to get worse if we kept talking. As we got to the ground Cody asked,

"You want to go chill by the pond?"

I responded, "Yeah, it's been a long day. Chilling would be nice." We walked towards the pond.

"Do you want sugar?" Cody asked

I responded,

"Do I, I haven't eaten all day. Where did you get it?"

"From the plane. I have plenty," he spoke. He handed me a candy packet full of Swedish Fish. The Swedish Fish tasted amazing. The taste reminded me of a home I couldn't place, but it felt familiar. It was one sweet thing, on a bitter day.

"Do you want any?" I asked.

He responded, "No, Ralph fed me well."

The thought of Ralph being generous, gave me chills. He was a monster, no matter what good he did for people.

The rainforest was more beautiful every time I walked through it. I saw the beautiful bloomed bushes and the lush grass with a wide variety of colored flowers. Trees that were very huge with green leaves. The trees provided a canopy over most of the island.

When we got to the pond, Cody asked, "You want to see what you can do with your power."

"That would be fun," I spoke, "what do you want me to do?"

He spoke, "I don't know, anything."

I thought of what to do. Then, I had it.

"Okay," I said, "I got it."

Cody spoke, "Take my breath away."

I concentrated. I stared down at the grass. The grass was lush and green. I put my hand down, and slowly lifted it, rotating my palm up slowly. The grass ripped out of the ground. Each strand individually rose. Each strand floated as my hand rose. They rose at the same pace as my hand. The grass floated to my shoulder height. The grass spun in circles. Hundreds of these strands swirled in a spread-out pattern. I commanded seeds around me to do the same. The seeds rose from the trees and shot towards me. They swirled in the air. It surprised me, I was able to do it so easily. "That is so cool!" Cody exclaimed.

"Thanks," I responded, "Watch this." I reached my hand toward the ground. A round long stick shook. It jumped, then it levitated. It levitated up above my head, then it shot towards Cody. It sat now on top of Cody's head. I concentrated all of my focus on that stick. The grass fell to the ground.

"What are you doing?" Cody asked.

"Just wait," I responded.

"What are you doing?" Cody asked.

"Just wait," I responded. Something formed around the top of Cody's head. It wrapped around his head. A hat quickly formed around his head. The cap fit him perfectly. His face lit up. His eyes shimmered and got big. The cap looked good on him.

"That is cool," Cody exclaimed.

"Now we can put a coonskin over that if we find any coons. It will feel great," I offered. I levitated the cap off of his head, then I held it. I imagined a c indented into the smooth, white wood. The wood obeyed as I thought

"Look at it," I said.

Cody peered down at the hat. His eyes shimmered and went bright. "THAT IS SO COOL! Thanks!

A c for Cody," he celebrated.

I was lost in the ease of the moment. Making one person happy, changed my mood. I thought about why it was so easy. Up on the mountain and when I battled the snake, I thought all my power came from my anger. The only time I could use it was when I was ready to explode. When I constructed the tree house, I was calm, and it happened almost effortlessly. Here it was the same thing. Then it hit me. My emotions did drive my power, but chaos made it hard to focus. Anger wasn't the most powerful source... a calm mind was.

Just then, I saw a bush in front of us move. It spun to face it, ready to fight.

"Who is that?" I asked.

A boy ran out of a bush. It was Jason. "Hey guys," he spoke as he panted.

"Why are you here," I asked.

He responded, "I ran from Ralph. He is a murderer. I thought I might go back home if I went with him, but he is psycho."

"Anyone with you?" Cody asked.

"No," he responded, "I was also afraid of Ralphs power, but when I saw what you could do, I had faith."

"Hey welcome home," Cody exclaimed. Jason asked forgiveness, "George, sorry I hung you by the tree."

I spoke, "No problem. He forced you. I heard you try to refuse."

Jason said, "I am sorry you have to go through this. Jacks death broke my heart. Someone that cruel deserves no friends."

"Why are you guys over here?" Jason asked.

"Everyone hates us for letting Jack die," Cody responded.

"That wasn't your fault," Jason exclaimed.

I responded, "Exactly. Thank you."

Jason spoke, "People in distress don't think clearly. They let emotion contradict their decisions."

"Yeah. They think we are so horrible," Cody responded.

"Hopefully, we can fix that. It's good to be home," Jason added.

Chapter Twelve

The next thing I knew was I was in a bed. White sheets formed like a pillow around my body. I felt like I was in heaven. Then, I noticed, I wore a blue hospital robe.

I jerked my arm, wanting to get out of my bed, but something restrained me. Steel bars held my legs and arms. Somebody did not want me to leave.

I was in a whitewashed room. Metal trays lined both sides of the bed. Medical equipment I had never seen before, was all around me. I couldn't remember my past, but I knew I had never seen technology this advanced. A capsule that reached back into the wall, was directly ahead of me. The room had windows to my left. The window looked out to a hallway. A door to the hallway was ahead to the left.

A woman stood at the foot of the bed. She held a device and was typing away on it, almost unaware that I was watching. She spoke, "Justine, send me the." I couldn't exactly understand what the last words she said were.

I shook, trying to get away. A small clear pearl, exactly the same as mine appeared on top of the device. She walked over to a tray and started to manipulate the pearl. I shook the bars, and I knew she could hear me.

I tried to talk. My mouth moved, but nothing came out. The woman was looking at me. I pointed at my mouth. "You are wondering why you can't talk?" the woman chided, "You've been drugged. It makes the procedure easier. You can move your mouth as much as you want, but you can't talk."

The woman walked over to a panel with an opening at the center and what seemed to be a thousand little fingers. It appeared to be made of steel. She placed the pearl inside the slot, in between a bundle of the steel fingers. The device came to life and locked down on the pearl.

The woman picked up a device on that same tray and clicked a button. The tray rolled over.

She went to the panel and pulled a lever to the right of the pearl. The pearl moved forward out of the panel. She picked up the large device and set it on my lap. She sat the pearl in my lap as well. The device was heavy. My bed automatically raised up, so I was sitting up. The fingers on the steel device reached forward and clamped onto my head. I felt like my head was being crushed.

The pain was excruciating, and I started to shake. My mind felt like it was being torn apart. I saw wisps of energy coming out of my forehead. The pearl filled up with a swirl of colors. I jerked and twisted, but it was no use. I lost all control. I felt life itself being sucked out of my body. I shook and screamed in agony, but nothing come out of my mouth.

Suddenly, everything went hazy. I felt sleepy. I could barely see or move. I was lifeless. My body felt limp and I could barely think. Even trying to focus was hard. I felt the blackness closing in.

I woke up. I was breathing heavily, muscles clenched. It was a dream, but it seemed so real. I rubbed my eyes.

I forgot I had fallen asleep. It had been a few nights since we found Jason. That dream had felt so real. I had felt pain. My mind was in pain and I held my head as if I was still in the dream. Whatever that was, it felt like that machine was about to kill me.

I sat up staring at the hemlock wood that made up the treehouse. "I knew you would wake up," a voice offered. I heard wood creaking. It was the sound of someone getting out of bed. I looked to my right. Cody was sitting up. His eyes were red as if he had been up all night. "Have you been watching me at night.?" I asked.

Cody whispered, "I can't sleep. You are up all night. You go to sleep, then you wake up locked in a nightmare. You scream in your dreams, and no matter what I do, I can't wake you. Sometimes, you get up, then collapse. What do you see in your dreams?"

"Sorry, I didn't realize."

"It's no problem, what's going on in your dreams. I've been thinking about it a lot." Cody said.

"What do you mean?" I asked.

"I see you wake up, then you can't go back to sleep, because you are terrified. It's your past. I think you are getting wisps of your past through dreams."

"You might be right. I can control my body in my dreams." I said

"Exactly! You are going somewhere between a dream and your past. Your subconscious is replaying your past."

"Do they feel almost too real?" he asked.

"Yeah, most of my dreams are a grayer color. The colors in these dreams are vivid. It's almost more colorful and real, like reality. I usually just forget my dreams, but these stick with me for days as I try to understand them."

Cody said, "Well with my dreams the settings are almost always places I have been. With you, you don't know where you have been."

"When you wake up, just try to focus on breathing. That helps me sleep," Cody whispered.

I replied, "I try that. I have tried everything else. It keeps getting stuck in my head. I rubbed my eyes again. "I'm too tired to sleep," I said. I wanted to get out of my bed. The pain in that dream that had felt so real bugged me.

"You seemed concerned about going back to sleep?" Cody added.

I responded, "It's just that the pain. The pain was so excruciating and real. The pearl that I have was also in the dream. It felt like my life was getting sucked out of me and going into the pearl."

"Do you think your power would have been restored if you touched it?" he asked.

"That is what I am thinking," I whispered.

Cody spoke back, "Well maybe before you go to bed you think about bright things. Try to think about how good life is and how beautiful the island is, and the fact that we have Jason."

I drifted from Cody's words, into instant pain. My body fell to the ground, and I found myself standing in an alleyway, I didn't recognize. Skyscrapers were everywhere. It was night, but lights shone all across the city as if it were daytime. Metal dumpsters rolled around on their side. Garbage was everywhere. A large garbage bin was to my right. An industrial brick factory was behind me. A building that looked like it was entirely made of glass, was in front of me. The sun was setting across town, and it was getting cold. I was standing on a thick, dirty patch of concrete, concerned about what would come next.

A silhouette appeared at the end of the alleyway. As I turned to look at him, he disappeared. He literally went up into a cloud of black dust, as if he were never there.

I saw a boy that appeared much older than me. He wore blue shorts with a gray shirt and long black socks. His hair was brown and wavy, like mine.

As I looked at him, he was staring back at me, with anger and vengeance in his eyes. It was the same way I had looked at Ralph when he killed Jack. This teenager was furious with me.

Bolts of energy surged out of his fingertips. Long bolts of yellow and blue lighting soared through the air. I snapped back, realizing I was in trouble, but it was too late. I could barely see the bolts, as they snapped through the air, towards me. I was too late to respond, and I took the blow, directly to the stomach. I shot back, and hit the wall behind me, like a cannonball. The wall gave way, and bricks fell down on me.

Suddenly, I was back. I was in the tree house. Cody knelt on the ground. He was staring intently at me. I was breathing heavily.

"Are you okay?" Cody asked.

"Yeah, I am okay."

Cody looked at me, "What happened?"

"I flashed into another dream. It was someone I must have known in my past, because he looked familiar."

"Who was it," Cody inquired.

"I don't know a friend, brother? I definitely knew him. Please drop it for now."

I had a real headache from that mini dream.

"Fine," he responded.

"Maybe we should get to bed," Cody spoke.

"Yeah," I responded. I got up and walked over to my bed. I plopped myself on the down and got myself comfortable. I stared up at the ceiling, scared of what might come, and now it wasn't just Ralph I was afraid of.

Chapter Thirteen

I woke up the next day, feeling well rested, and Jason, Cody and I went over to the pond. Everyone was still angry at us. I spent the day with them.

The jungle was gorgeous today, and I could feel its energy. It had rained yesterday, but today was nice and hot. White puffy clouds were scattered across the sky. Flowers started to peak, out and I could tell today would be a nice day. The water was cool, refreshing and glistened in the sun. We dove in and swam across the pond, to cool off. The water felt good.

We challenged each other, racing back and forth across the pond. One end of the pond, to the other, to see who was the fastest. Jason was the fastest swimmer, with perfect form and moved through the water, like a dolphin. We would try to beat him, and he would let us get ahead, but at the very end, he would come flying past us. Swimming took my mind off the dreams. I felt at ease. The trees swayed, and the water was clear.

I washed my clothes on the gray rocks. My clothes had never been cleaner. I scrubbed them as much as I could.

There was a nice breeze, and we lay soaking up the sun. Suddenly, the ground shook. I rolled over and opened my eyes, only to have someone crash down on top of me. The ground shook, and was collapsing in on itself, and pulling us with it. Cody was terrified, as we struggled to climb out.

The ground started to shake even worse as if it would come apart at its core. I managed to get away and I rolled over onto a grassy patch. I was covered in dirt and could barely see. "So much for washing my clothes," I complained.

"George, I can't get up," Cody spoke, as he rolled, trying to get away.

"I know," I responded.

"George, do something?" Jason begged.

"I'm not sure I can stop an earthquake," I moaned.

"Please, help? I can't hold on!" Jason snapped.

"Okay," I said. I knew I had to do something to get us out of this.

"Sure, take your time!" Jason mumbled.

Cody grunted, "Can you guys shut up for once and help?"

I felt the grass on my fingertips. "Grow," I spoke. The grass immediately grew out in long strands and circled around my hands. It covered up every inch of my fingers, making them look like gloves.

I held on tight and moved the gloves into the air. I pulled free of the ground. I was barely off the ground and I imagined the same for Jason and Cody. Grass grew around both of Jason and Cody's hands. The grass slowly moved around their fingers. I heard a huge crack. "George, hurry," Cody hollered.

"I am working on it," I responded. Then, I looked around. The quake broke a tree right next to them. The tree was about to come crashing down on them.

I tried to pull him up with the grass. I relaxed and concentrated, but I couldn't get him to move. I wasn't sure why I couldn't move him, so I focused on the tree that was about to crush them. "No," I heard Cody scream.

I would not let another friend perish. I pushed my arms forward and ripped the tree out of the ground. I threw it to the other side of the pond. Jason and Cody scrambled up and out of the churning sand, and for the first time could see what was happening.

"Oh no," Cody spoke.

"What?" Jason asked.

Cody responded, "I think I know what is causing the earthquake," he said while looking at me.

I knew what he meant, I said, "You don't think there might be another?"

"Oh, this thing isn't the same. This thing has to be colossal. At least ten times larger." The ground rumbled like an earthquake, every couple seconds. I heard trees exploding, and what sounded like colossal footsteps, causing the earth to tremble. Suddenly, we heard a deep roar of a lion, that made the trees bend.

"What do you think it is?" I asked.

"I think we are about to find out," Jason responded.

The bellowing roar got more menacing by the second. We knew the sound we were hearing, was the footsteps of some giant beast.

I pleaded "Please don't be a snake." We took off, running towards the treehouse. The footsteps were getting closer, and the sound grew louder. We lost our footing, over and over, because of the quaking of the ground. Giant pine trees in a distance crashed to the ground like dominoes. I knew this wasn't an earthquake. The roar was terrifying and deep. I wanted to turn back, hop on a boat and head to Jersey, but there was no boat. I had to try to save our friends. We ran as fast as we could.

They could already be dead. We couldn't see it yet but could smell the warm stink of its breath in the air. It had to be close. Too close. We darted towards the treehouse and climbed. I climbed, branch by branch. "Hey, we've got to go!" I yelled. No response. We continued to climb. We reached the top and jumped into the treehouse. I screamed, "Something giant is coming. We have to run."

"You liar. You are just trying to get attention," Chris responded. They heard the noise, and felt the shaking, but had been playing a loud game, and dismissed the danger.

"You are all liars," Stacy spoke.

Jason spoke up, "You guys. George is a great guy and is trying to save you. We half to leave, or we are all going to die."

Still angry about Jack, they refused, and offered "If he couldn't save Jack, how is he going to save all of us? We are going to stay right here, where it is safe."

Jason screamed "You are going to get us all killed!"

Chris yelled back, "I'd rather be here than trust him."

I grabbed Jason, and said, "Thanks Jason, but this isn't working."

"What do we do," he responded.

"They won't listen, so I am going to have to stop whatever this is before it gets here." I brought out my carving.

Cody stated, "George, you can't. This thing is not like the snake. You heard its roar. You heard and saw the destruction."

"I have to try," I responded. I pressed the smooth button on my carving. It transformed into my round lit shield. I walked towards the ladder to the second story.

Right as I grabbed the first handle on the ladder, Chris grabbed my arm. He said, "Don't die." I didn't know if he was being sarcastic, but I didn't have time for a fight. I climbed up to the second story of the tree house.

I looked up at the roof and concentrated. I took deep breaths to stay calm, knowing I would need all my power to survive this. The roof cracked. A circle of wood fell down to the floor. I jumped up, grabbed the roof. I pulled myself up.

I looked down to see what was destroying the forest. I couldn't believe what I saw. I didn't have to look down this beast was colossal. It was almost as big as the mountain itself.

It had the mane of a lion. The mane was full and coarse. It had the majestic white wings of an eagle, but the head looked to be of a thick-haired man. I said it, out loud to myself, "It has a man's head!" It was still way off, but it turned, and I could see it had a serpent for a tail. Its head was pale, and dirty, with black eyes. The beast was massive and strong. It stocked forward, like an attacking bulldog.

"What is it?" Cody asked from beneath.

I responded, "I don't know." I continued to stare at the beast. How would I fight this thing?

It bellowed, "*FOUR THOUSAND YEARS OF DEEP SLEEP, NOW MORTALS, DISTURB MY SLUMBER! WHERE ART THOU? COME OUT AND FACE YOUR DOOM!"*

"What are you?" I whispered.

It bellowed again, "*WHERE ART THOU BLOODY MORTAL?*" This beast was colossal, elephantine. I couldn't fight something this big. My power would not be enough. I concentrated, trying to come up with a plan." Breathe, just breathe," I muttered.

I had to get closer and keep it away from the treehouse. The thought came, and I felt the wood beneath my feet shooting into the air. The wood was swirling. It wrapped around my feet, and I shot into the air. I was flying!

I was moving at an incredible speed, and this gave me confidence. I was shooting through the air. I twisted and spun, testing my agility. The wind blew hard against my face as I moved towards the beast. I flailed, my arms and yelled.

I flew straight past the giant head of the beast and landed on its shoulders, behind its massive neck. Each strand of hair was as big as my body. I looked around for a weakness or an idea. "**WHAT IS ON ME? GET OFF ME, AND SHOW YOURSELF,**" it spoke. It occurred to me that it might be best, not to fight, but to reason with it.

Suddenly, the animal shook. It was trying to buck me off. I lost concentration and bounced, rolled, then plummeted off its back.

First, I panicked, while flailing my arms. I saw the trees on the way down. I thought breath just breath. I focused.

Immediately, I felt something grab my hand. I used a branch to reach up, and catch my hand, in order to slow my fall. I landed gently on the ground and turned towards it.

"*OVER HERE!*" I hollered. The beast turned around. It was glaring at me, like a tiny ant.

I stood terrified, and shaking, with my shield in hand. I felt small and powerless against this beast even with my shield.

It spoke, "**YOU DARE COME TO THIS ISLAND TO CHALLENGE ME!**"

I hadn't challenged this beast. What was it talking about? The breath of the beast almost sucked me off the ground. I roared back at it "What do you mean? I haven't challenged you.".

"*YOU LIER!*" the beast hollered, blowing me off my feet.

I spoke, "Why does everything on this island want to kill me?" Its mountainous claw looked like a tree stabbed into the ground. Suddenly, it swung at me. I tried to move, but it was too fast and too big.

The orange-furred claw was coming. I froze in my tracks, stunned. I was caught again in an incredible situation, on a beautiful island, fighting for my life. I couldn't process what was happening. The claw crashed down on me, with the force of 10 trains.

It hit me and shot me high into the air. The impact made me feel like I had multiple broken bones.

As I flew, I could feel power shooting through me. I was hurt, but calm and fearless. I came, crashing down. My back hit the tree. My head hit the ground first, then my body whiplashed to the ground. I came to a stop, in a lump.

I couldn't breathe. Blood clogged my mouth, again. I could feel blood running down my back, from the impact. I was sore, but I could feel myself starting to heal, and my head cleared almost instantly. I jumped to my feet again, like an ant in front of an elephant.

"***STRONG MORTAL, YOU ARE!***" the beast said.

"What do you want?" I asked.

The beast responded, "**I AM THE MIGHTY BEAST OF OLD. I WAS WOKEN FROM MY FOUR-THOUSAND YEAR SLEEP, BY YOUR THUNDERINGS. THIS IS A SERIOUS OFFENSE.**"

I could not compete with this Sphinx. I had to try to stop this crazy thing. I reached out my hand with a thought. I concentrated all my power on the trees. The trees around me started to rumble. They wouldn't come free. I concentrated and tried to relax. I thought of the people that needed me, even if they didn't believe in me yet.

A full-grown hemlock tree shot out of the ground. The roots ripped out. Parts of the tree fell. The tree formed into a straight shaft, with a hardened sharp blade on one side. I grunted, and screamed as I moved the tree up higher, and higher.

The Sphinx was still considering me. He turned to attack again. I sent the blade. The giant wooden knife raced down, towards The Great Sphinx's tail. Like a sword, it sliced through the tail of the beast. It roared as its tail plummeted to the ground. The blade stabbed into the earth, with an earth-shaking impact. Dirt and dust flew up from the chaos.

The Sphinx cried out, "*Meta. I SHOULD HAVE KNOWN. WHO ARE YOU?*"

I responded, "Meta?"

"*DON'T PLAY GAMES WITH ME, BOY.*"

"What is a Meta?" I asked.

The beast bellowed, "*DID THE TRAITOR SEND YOU?*" It confused me. He knew something, and I didn't care who or what he was. I wanted to know. I threw my shield at its head. The shield hit with a tremendous force but bounced off and fell to the ground.

"*DON'T TRY FIGHTING. EVEN THE ORIGINAL META'S THAT WERE CONSIDERED IDOL'S COULD NOT DEFEAT ME!*" The Great Sphinx spoke.

"What are you talking about?" I asked.

"**HOW DO YOU NOT KNOW?**" The Great Sphinx asked.

I proposed, "I have no memory of anything in my past. As far as I know, I have been alive for a few months."

"*INTERESTING,*" The Great Sphinx spoke.

I didn't want to fight this thing, and I wasn't sure I would live through the battle. I had to find an answer. I asked, "Can I do anything to repair the offense of waking you from your slumber?"

The Sphinx responded, "**ONE THING I GAVE META'S OVER THE AGES, WERE CERTAIN RIDDLES. IN ORDER TO SURVIVE MY WRATH, YOU MUST ANSWER MY RIDDLE. ANSWER IT WRONG, AND YOU AND EVERYONE AROUND YOU DIES.**"

I stared at The Great Sphinx, confidently, then I replied, "Okay!"

The Sphinx took a deep breath, which again, almost sucked me off the ground. Then he whispered, "**WHAT IS THAT, WHICH IN THE MORNING GOES UPON FOUR, UP ON TWO FEET IN THE AFTERNOON, AND IN THE EVENING, UPON THREE?**"

I was not good at riddles, and it was hard to understand what he had said. I asked The Great Sphinx to repeat. I had no idea, what answer to offer. I whispered, "What is that which in the morning that goes up on four feet, up on two feet in the afternoon, and in the evening, upon three." I turned it over and over in my mind, trying to make the connection. He offered that no one had ever answered correctly. All had gone to their deaths. I whispered the riddle over again, and again, and again.

My friend's lives depended on a stupid riddle. The Great Sphinx constantly rolled its eyes at me, impatient, because of the time I was taking. I tried to force the thought into my mind. Tears started to roll down my face, and I started to lose confidence. I really wanted to head for home, wherever that was.

"**GIVE UP, YOU HAVE FAILED,**" The Sphinx bellowed.

I responded, "Just a little more time."

"*NO!*" it responded. The mouth of The Great Sphinx was coming at me. The glossy white teeth looked like they had not eaten in ages. Its breath smelled like a thousand years of rot. I saw the teeth only inches away.

Just as he was ready to bite down, I yelled, "MAN!" The Great Sphinx stopped. It brought it's head back. The eyes of The Great Sphinx stared at me in awe. "*WHY*?" it asked.

I answered, "Man because when you're a baby you crawl on four. When you're an adult you walk on two, and when you're old, you walk with a cane, and that makes three."

The Sphinx broke into a grin, "**AFTER THOUSANDS OF YEARS OF RIDDLES! NO MAN HAS EVER ANSWERED CORRECTLY, EXCEPT YOU. JUST DO ME A FAVOR, CHILD. TRY NOT TO CAUSE SO MUCH RUCKUS. I WON'T BE SO GENEROUS IF YOU WAKE ME AGAIN. I SEE YOU'RE DESTINED FOR SOMETHING MUCH LARGER THAN I.**"

The tailless Sphinx turned and bolted away, kicking up rocks and dirt, as it raced towards the mountain. The earth shook, with each step, and my heart slowed as he disappeared. As suddenly as it started, this beautiful world fell silent again. I sat down, knowing I should get back to the others, but it could wait. I felt uneasy about the future but capable of handling almost anything. I made the grass push up under me, like a giant pillow. I laid under the trees and just felt the breeze. The guys could wait.

Chapter Fourteen

Weeks passed with no drama, monsters, or psychopaths. I helped with hunting every day. Days would pass with no food. There seemed to be an ebb and flow with the animals on the island as if they all went into hiding at the same time. Eventually, that would end and there would be plenty of food again. Life was difficult, and my power helped, but not that much.

I had been badly hurt in my encounter with the Sphinx. I was bruised, almost everywhere. I had broken bones and lacerations down my back and legs. I rested for many hours each day, trying to recover. Even with my supernatural healing, the pains seemed to stay. I still hunched a bit when I walked. I was getting better and stronger every day.

Days seemed to pass by slowly, and even though there were a lot of us, I felt lonely. Island life was hard, and you had to keep up with things. I was always musing about what The Great Sphinx had said, "You are destined for greater things than even I." I wondered what he meant. In the middle of all of this, we were still kids and there was a lot of murmuring and bickering.

I mastered being able to start a fire, using my powers, and on one night I made a massive bonfire, using my new skills. Each night we would make a fire, and everyone would tell old stories and memories.

We had good times but staying on the island was boring. We eventually had played every game we could think of. Days of no food made people grumpy, and sometimes I had to be the one keeping everyone together.

Jason was a funny guy and always knew how to make us laugh. We tried to do something different every night, but soon we ran low on ideas and stories.

We spent some time, dealing with the dead serpent. It was so large, I didn't consider the consequence of its death, until weeks after the battle. The beast smelled horrid, and the wind would carry the smell to our camp and drown us in it.

We came up with a plan to dispose of it. We hiked to the back side of the island, where none of us had been. I then spent a day making two of the largest trees we could find. I grew them to about 200 feet tall. The next day, we hiked across the island to the serpent. All the while we walked, I caused a bundle of roots from the two trees to grow and follow us.

Once we were within 100 yards of the snake, I commanded the roots to wrap around its body. With all my power, I then caused the roots to contract over the miles and drag the snake to the other side of the island. It was massive and sapped my strength, so it took two days to get back. Once it was by the beach, I wrapped it in beams and rolled it into the ocean, and out to sea, where the sea life would devour it. It was hard work, but a good distraction, and I learned a lot about using my powers.

Each night I had the same dream of the jungle in a conflagration. I heard voices in the dark coming from outside every night.

I started to develop insomnia, and I was paranoid about Ralph killing another one of us. I constantly looked at the mountain, wondering what the other teenagers were doing. I was too paranoid to sleep because I would watch out the treehouse in case Ralph showed up. He never came, but I still could not sleep. Losing sleep did not help my feelings about staying on the island.

It was afternoon, I was completely healed, and everyone was out doing their own activities. I was standing on the roof of the tree house with Jason. I offered, "Hey what do you say we climb up to the top of the hemlock tree? You could see the waterfall and the sea from up there."

Jason shuddered "Uhhhhhhh, are you sure that's safe?" His eyes were wide and large, and looked like a puppies, when it wanted food.

"Come on, princess!" I called, already climbing up the tree.

As we climbed, Jason spoke, "Are you sure this is safe?"

I responded, "Don't worry. If you fall, I'll catch you."

"Okay," he responded. The top of the hemlock was at least twenty feet up from the top of the tree house. As we climbed, I screamed, "Aggh, I'm falling!" Jason screamed in fright, then saw that I was fine. "Don't scare me like that that, you jerk!"

When we got to the top of the tree, I reached down, toward the branches. I focused my power, and soon the branches made one circular area to sit on. We sat down, gazing out at the seashore.

Waves crashed onto the beach. The grains of sand made of black and tan with the waves crashing against them looked gorgeous. The sea looked endless. Debris splashed onto the shore. There were no islands in sight, which made me feel even more remote.

I asked, "Jason, what was the world outside this like?" as he spoke, I shifted to face him.

"Well, there is school and the sports, and."

"No. I mean what did you like to do?"

Jason responded, "Well I was not so good at school. I was great at sports. I played football and basketball. I was center in basketball and left tackle for football. Everyone expects me to be like the other jocks. They were jerks though. They expected me to hang around them and act like them, in order for them to treat you, decent.

I never really had any friends that were good friends except my brother Chase. My dad was into sports, and my mom expected me to be amazing in school. I have never had a friend like you before. Especially with abilities.

"You've really not met anyone like me, because I can only remember living for like a few months, and I have met three of them, including me."

"I'm not even joking."

"What is the one thing you would want, besides going home?" I asked.

Jason responded, "Maybe just if Ralph were not here. It scares me to know someone is hunting us."

"Me too."

He spoke, "I can tell. I see you awake all night. It looks like your mind is racing."

"Yeah. After my brother died, I can't get over it. I could have saved him. I stay up, so I can protect you guys if he ever comes back."

"That is kind, but you don't have to do that."

I responded, "I know, but I feel like I was given this power for a reason. I am also very worried about what Ralph will do."

"One day everything will work out for all of us. We will all go home," Jason stated.

"I don't know where my home is. This is basically my life. I have a brother and another out there, but both want me dead."

"Bizarre," Jason stated.

"I will work something out. With my powers, I'm sure I can do something."

"I am sure you are right," Jason responded.

I stated, "I feel you. I wish there were a way we could just sail back home."

Jason asked, "Well, why not?"

"What do you mean?" I asked.

Jason spoke, "You're the one with the power to do it."

"Do what?" I asked.

He responded, "Build a boat. We have the leather from the airplane. We have enough to make a sail. Let the wind carry us somewhere."

"It is too risky," I responded.

"Too risky! It will be ages before people come, and who knows if they will even notice us.

You know I am right. It is worth a shot. If it does not work, we will have enough wood for you to levitate us back."

"That is true," I responded, "I like that plan."

Jason asked, "Are you serious?"

"Dead serious," I responded.

"Well then let's go tell the others." I stood up, and moved my hand, which pulled the platform from the top of the tree. We were levitating. We flew through the air on the wooden platform, and soon we were on the ground.

"That was wicked," Jason gasped. I laughed.

Jason spoke, "Seriously, if I had your power, I would put like wood on my shoes, and jump across an entire football field. I would fly around and just have fun." I chuckled.

We rounded everyone up. We were over by the pond. I had my feet dipped into the clear water. The water felt cool. "What was so important that you had to round everyone up," Chris asked.

I responded, "Jason had an idea, and it might just work. We want to try to build a boat and sail home."

Chris argued, "Say this works. What if we land in, say, Africa? How would we get back to the United States?"

I responded, "Well with my power I am sure we can figure something out."

Jason spoke, "It is risky, but if we sink or something destroys the boat, then George can fly us back to the island or safety."

"It is too risky," Christopher argued.

I spoke, "Face it, it's risky to stay. No one is coming, and Ralph will kill us if we stay."

"Okay," Cody agreed, and everyone responded in the affirmative.

I asked, "Are you serious?"

Cody spoke, "Let's do it."

We collected the leather, and we soon had enough. We got as many supplies of fruits and vegetables as we could find. We packed these in a large, sealed container, I formed out of a Hemlock tree. We loaded backpacks, with all the supplies we could carry.

We were ready to leave.

"It is crazy to think we are leaving," Cody said.

"Yeah," I responded.

Cody spoke, "It is good though."

"Yeah," I said. We headed off. The rainforest was calm as we walked. Everyone's faces were lit up with smiles. For the first time, everyone had hope in what was about to happen.

It was going to be a long hike, so we started to talk, as usual. The rainforest was interesting. The various tropical plants were starting to bloom, with a variety of flowers and colors. Cody and I cracked jokes at each other, and we talked.

"What did you like to do at home?" I asked.

Cody responded, "Well, I played basketball and track. I was good in school. I came from a family of four. Me, Mom, Dad, and my little sister Lidia."

"Cool. Did you get along with your sister?" I asked.

Cody responded, "Most of the time. Siblings always bicker, but we still always tried to be as nice as we could to each other."

We went on talking. I was desperate to know what would happen when I got out into the world. I tried to interact with everyone, so I could get to know them better.

We came across a buffalo, but even that couldn't kill my mood. It did not attack us, and I had no fear. The buffalo just stood its ground.

Stickers stuck into our socks. Grass scratched our legs. Bugs shot at our faces. It was early afternoon, and people were starting to get hungry. We needed to keep moving to get to the spot we had chosen.

Cody and I talked for most of the time. Cody was the person I got along with best. He always made the best of things. I prepared myself for the job ahead of me. They had never asked me to perform such a difficult task. I would have to use up all of my strength to form a boat right after I had walked for hours across the rainforest.

Hours passed of difficult terrain. Our legs were sore, and we all felt tired. We were all just about spent, having hauled our packs and the trunk all day, when we came over the top of the final hill. We were there. We were at the shore.

Debris washed up on the beach. The water looked blue. I felt good, but we were all tired. I was excited to leave but felt the burdens of leaving Ralph and his gang.

"Well build," Cody stated.

"Just wait for a second," I spoke. I sat on the ground.

"Are you going to sit there?" asked Stacy.

I spoke, "My legs hurt, and whenever I use my power, I am sore for a while after that. Just wait."

I closed my eyes and concentrated. I exerted all of my power into this process. I breathed deeply. My strength was low, and I needed to focus. This was the hardest thing I had done, yet, with my power.

I heard the trees ripping out of the soil. The trees flew but keeping them up in the air was difficult. I moved the trees that together weighed hundreds of thousands of pounds. I exerted all of my power. Soon, the cypress trees all dropped to the water. A colossal splash of water shot towards us. We all got wet.

Once they were in the water, it was easier. I brought all the trees together. The trees became smooth and stuck together. I started forming the boat in my mind. I formed the bottom deck. It took a second, but not too long to form the entire bottom floor. The walls rose up, and the top deck of the boat, developed with a rail.

It was floating in the waters. I now forced the boat onto the sandy shore partly. I kept working at it for an hour. Making rooms and Pushing up the masts. I didn't know that much about boats. Mainly, I added things I thought we would need. It was about 80 feet long and 40 feet wide when it was done. Not perfect but it looked sturdy.

I spoke, "Well, let's go."

I dropped a seed on the ground, and it reached out and wrapped around the bottom of my shoe. I levitated through the air. I dropped to the deck of the boat. Seeds I had found, were the easiest to manipulate. As if they had so much potential, they were bursting to do or be anything you asked. I carried a sack full of them for the trip, just in case.

Everyone else climbed aboard. As they walked the wood creaked. Wind shot at my face. My hair blew to the side.

I walked down the stairs to the bottom story. The stairs were in a tiny hallway down the center of the boat. The stairs were plain, but looked amazing, and were smooth and symmetrical. The color of the wood was a light brown.

I walked down and saw the bottom story. It was exactly as I imagined, but more perfect in person. A table sat in front of me in an open space. It matched the floor and steps. The table was long and rectangular. A counter was to my left. There were intricate designs on cabinets underneath for storage. All the wood in here was the same color. A mini basketball hoop was on the far side of the room. Two couches that made up a half of a rectangle to the far left of the room. The couches had nice and comfortable armrests and were just the perfect size. Chairs circled around the table.

"This is amazing," Cody blurted.

"Truly," I responded.

"Thank you," Cody applauded.

"Thank Jason," I responded.

"Thanks," Cody stated.

"No prob," Jason replied.

Everyone sat on the chairs and admired the room. The result surprised me.

"I have a good feeling about this," Jason stated.

"Me too," Chris responded.

"Well, I guess we should get going," I stated.

"Yeah," Chris spoke.

"Hey Chris, let's go set the sail," Cody ordered.

I walked up the stairs to see a beautiful railing all around the edge. I walked over to the railing. It was a nice, sturdy and tall, to keep us from going over the edge in a storm. The railing made the ship look unique.

A mist came towards my face. The ship rocked, but not much. I looked out over the horizon. I was ready to go home. The mast was huge, and possibly a little taller than it needed to be. Chris and Cody were setting the sail and had climbed up, to lash it in place. I hoped we knew enough, that things would be okay. Soon, the sail caught the wind. I forced the ship back into the water, and we moved out to sea, slowly.

I walked back down the hallway, and we were off to play. The main area below deck was a huge open space, with a 20-foot ceiling. The sport I liked the most was basketball which we played with a ball we wove out of a long stiff grass. It didn't bounce perfectly but it worked on an island and a boat. Chris, Christopher, and Cody played horse. I rested. I watched as Cody, Chris and Christopher played basketball.

My effort making the boat had sucked the life from me. I felt as if I could barely move a muscle. I laid down, trying to rest, while I watched the others.

I admired the game that Cody and the two Christophers were playing. As usual after building, I was hungry and wanted something to eat. We stored our fruit and vegetables in the cupboard.

"Hey, Stacy could you get me an apple?" I asked.

"Sure," she responded. Stacy looked into the cupboard, and she threw me an apple. I tried to catch it, but I missed, and it smashed into my chest. I took a large bite. The juicy red apple tasted great. The juice quenched my thirst.

Stacy and Isabella were playing chess on a board I had made before. It was a three-dimensional board with three-dimensional pieces. I watched as they played. I thought of ways that they each could win. They were terrible at the game, because they had never played. Somehow, I knew what the rules of Chess were.

Jason asked, "Anyone want to wrestle."

"I am good," I responded.

"Are you not man enough to do it?" he asked.

"I am not in the mood," I shot back with a faint smile. Jason ran at me. He accidentally hit the chess board which swept him off his feet. He crashed to the ground.

Cody stated, "I think George is too tough for you Jason."

"Shut up," Jason ordered. I chuckled. We played the day away with games. I played basketball games after I worked up the strength. I won a few times, but Cody won the most. He had a real talent for that sport. I eventually played chess, and I lost miserably.

Eventually I walked up on deck to watch our voyage. I peered out across the horizon. The wind was calm. Mist blew into the air, as the bow crashed against the waves. The sky was overcast, and rain was definitely going to come during the night.

A bucket was set out, so we could have fresh water. The bucket was big enough to sustain us for a while. As I stood on deck, I had hope that our lives were about to get better.

We all bedded down, with three men posted to guide the ship and watch for hazards. Sometime, after midnight it started to rain. We were down in the lower, large recreation room. Most of us had fallen asleep. I was resting on the cold hard floor. My brass carving was set next to me. I stared at it as the night went on. Eventually everyone but me was asleep. Thunder boomed, and the soothing sound of rain was all I could hear. I tossed and turned. I fiddled with my carving, but I could not fall asleep. Even with the exhaustion, sleep wouldn't come. I tried different positions, but I was still awake. I was hungry, but I did not feel like getting up.

As the night went on, I realized I would not be falling asleep. I opened the cupboard, and I grabbed a red, juicy apple. I plopped on the couch, and I ate my apple. I thought of what a real home might be like. I slowly ate the apple and tried to imagine the home, I couldn't remember. My mind drifted…

I awoke early, feeling much better. I went up to the main deck, and over to the railing, where I watched the sunrise. The bucket of water was full. My power focused on a stick on the deck. It soon formed into a small cup. I got water from the bucket and poured it in the cup. The water was refreshing.

The colors of the sky were pink, purple and orange. It was gorgeous. The water was calm, but the boat still seemed to rock back and forth. Mist sprayed in my face. I peered out over the sea. We could still see the island, but it had to be hundreds of miles away. We were going to make it, and the plan was working.

As we left the island, my mind had caught on the thought of all the kids we were leaving with that killer, Ralph. I had left them to die on the island. My brother, I had left to die. Even if he wanted to kill me, I still should have considered he wanted to leave. I felt like a failure, and a coward, leaving those kids to fend for themselves, with no powers.

The waves started to pick up, but the water barely got on deck. I was wet, but I didn't mind. The water washed off the dirt on my body. We were moving at a good pace, and certainly, we would find something within a few days.

I walked back down the stairs. I rested a little. I sat on the couch for a while, thinking of what to do. The boat was photographically memorized, front to back in my mind, so it felt like a dull and boring place.

I tried to find something to do. I concentrated my power. I closed my eyes. I envisioned what I wanted. The wood formed a climbing wall. Handholds were only in certain places, I had to jump to. I was short, so the twenty-foot ceiling was a tall climb.

I jumped onto the climbing wall. I jumped to each handhold. I heard a crack. I was focused on climbing, so I ignored the noise. The handholds were firm, but small. I was good at climbing, because of all the weeks of climbing, up and down the trees in the jungle. I heard more crackling and snapping, but I was still focused on the climb.

The next thing I knew I was falling. I was not the only thing that was falling. The climbing wall was falling, too. I hit the bottom of the ship, with a large crack. The climbing wall crashed into the hull and kept going. There was now a large hole in the ship.

My foot had gone through the hull and was stuck in the water. Wood splinters stabbed into my feet. I was sure, I was bleeding again. "Of-course, exactly on my streak of not messing up!" The hull wedged against my leg and made it hard to pull my leg out.

I focused my power, and relaxed. The wood stretched, and I pulled my foot out of the water. Blood immediately streamed onto the bow. Splinters cut my leg, and my foot and leg felt like it was on fire. I looked at my leg and moved all the splinters out of my skin, at once, in a quick painful movement. They fell to the floor.

Water was flooding the room. "Oh crap," I spoke. Water was up to my ankles and rising. "They are so going to hate me for this." I concentrated my power, and the hole filled in. Water was still in the room, but it was not flooding anymore.

"That was close." I was glad, I had stopped the flooding. That could have been horrible. I walked back to the chairs, relieved that that hadn't been worse. What would have happened if I couldn't have stopped the flooding.

I suddenly was aware of snapping and cracking, all around me. My leg cracked through the floor and slipped into the water below. We were sinking. I quickly, understood. I had used so much wood in the climbing wall, that it had thinned the wood in the ship too much. It wasn't strong enough to support us, or the force of the waves. We were in trouble. I got up. My other leg crashed through into the water. Every step I took, the wood was too thin, it broke. I yelled to everyone. "We are sinking! Get to the upper deck, now." The wood was cracking. "Oh, I am the worst." Water spilled into the room. Now, it was up above my waist.

I dove underwater and swam to the stairs. I was in my clothes and shoes, which made swimming difficult. It infuriated me, and I knew I caused this problem, and now we were in danger, again.

I was almost getting sucked into the water. What had I done? I had ruined our chance to get back home. Finally, I made it to the stairs. I moved up the stairs, cautiously being careful not to break through them. Cody bumped into me, and spoke, "Oh, hey early riser. You should work on less crappy situations."

I spoke, "Not now. We need to go back."

"Back where?" he asked.

"The island," I informed.

"Why? Can't you just fill it back up," he asked.

"No, that just made it worse," I spoke, "we lost too much material!"

Jason asked, "Can you shut up and go? We are sinking here!"

"Okay," I responded.

"I will tell the others. You make things you can control to fly back to the island," commanded Cody.

"Okay," I responded.

I walked over to the rail of the boat. All The rails around the boat were still thick and stout. I broke them all off the deck together. I pulled them in towards me. The deck was stripped of its railing, which made it very difficult, not to fall over the side. I wove the rails together, over and over mixing them with the seeds I had brought.

I formed the wood into, long, reclined chairs. These chairs looked like mini couches, with a large strap on each one. Each could only fit one of us. There were barely enough seats for everyone. Just as I finished, the last of the kids came out onto the deck.

"WHAT DID YOU DO!" Chloe hollered, "I WOKE UP, CLINGING TO THE WOOD ON THE BOW."

I exclaimed, "I know, I know, I know, Im sorry."

Cody ordered, "Get on the seats, now!"

The water was now at the deck. I sat in a chair, as everyone else did. I yelled to everyone to be as quiet as possible. I closed my eyes and started to breath. The chairs shook, then they levitated. Soon, we were flying. I flew high, so we could see the island. As soon as I saw it, I increased our speed, heading back to the island."

I felt like I was being drained of my power, at a rapid pace. I hoped I was strong enough to make it. The exertion made my bones ache, and my ears were starting to ring. My entire body started to give out. I had to get us back to the island. I had created this mess, and I had to fix what I done. It was my responsibility. I looked around, and everyone seemed to be enjoying the ride, and didn't realize the danger they were in. Much more of this, and we would all be in the water, and too far away from the island to swim. Cody started talking to me. He talked about his home and his friends, and I could feel myself starting to relax.

We raced forward, as I focused on his voice. We were getting closer to the island. We were starting to lose altitude, but I knew I could make it. It had only been around ten minutes, but I was almost completely drained. We came in fast, and hit the water, about 50 yards from the beach. The chairs hit the water and flipped violently. We all tumbled awkwardly in the sea. Everyone seemed to be okay, and immediately started swimming, *and yelling at me*. I tried to keep my head above water, but the blackness surrounded me like a blanket, and pulled me under.

Chapter Fifteen

I awoke in the rainforest. I was bouncing around, and I could feel the light from above, shooting over my eyelids, every so often. I could hear the crickets and animals, but also heavy breathing, right next to me. I opened my eyes and found myself almost lifeless. We were back in the jungle, under the canopy, and the sun was high, shooting through the gaps to the jungle floor. The trees swayed, and the wind blew. I could hear them, crunching through the leaves, as they followed the same path, we had walked, a couple days earlier. They noticed I was awake, and they immediately showed their disgust. "Today on George screws the pooch," Jason mumbled.

"I know," I responded. I was being carried in a hammock-like bed. It had two poles under both sides of me. Someone had wrapped the poles with gray leather. I was being carried on a makeshift stretcher.

I felt horrible and was exhausted. My vision was blurry. I could barely move my mouth, and I was numb almost everywhere. My hearing was the only thing intact. "Where are we going?" I slurred.

Stacy responded, "The tree house. That is where we live now."

I stated, "We can try the boat again."

"Not with you," Stacy responded.

"Guys, I know. I screwed up with Ralph. I screwed up with Jack and now this," I stated.

"And more," Isabella stated.

"Maybe you should try it," I retorted.

Cody stated, "Look George. You tried your hardest. You just need more time to master your skills."

"I know," I responded.

Stacy blurted, "Well it seems like you don't."

"What could I do to make things better?" I asked.

Stacy blabbered, "Stay out of our way, and stop almost getting us killed."

"Noted," I mumbled.

Stacy ordered, "Get up and walk on your own." I rolled to the side of the hammock, swung my feet over the side and stood up. I took a step, then I fell face first to the dirt. I had no control over my body. "Put him back in," Chris blurted.

Cody said, "Put him back in. George used all his strength to fly us back." Chris and Jason lifted me up and plopped me on the hammock. The travel back went by quickly, and with very little conversation. I was asleep most of the time. I was in a mini coma for almost 24 hours, before waking.

The next day, we finally made it back to our makeshift home. We all stood, looking up at the soaring hemlock that was our tree house. I had regained some of my strength, so I slowly climbed up the tree house and into the top story. I plopped myself on the couch.

"Do you guys want to go swimming?" Chris asked.

Cody stated, "No, I have had enough trouble with water in the past few days." Everyone piled out of the tree house, except Cody. Christopher peeked his head in, "You coming too, Cody?" he asked.

"I better take care of George," he stated.

"Okay," Chris spoke. Cody walked upstairs.

He walked beside the couch. "What do you need?" he asked.

I said, "To be honest. I am starving. Some food and water would be great."

"Okay," he responded. Cody climbed down to the bottom story. He soon came up with an apple. He threw the apple in the air towards me. I caught the apple. "There's your apple. I will get you some water."

I responded, "Thanks." I still didn't consider apples food. They were at best, a snack, but I would eat anything right now.

Our food had sunk with the ship, so the trip back was difficult. I ate the juicy apple. My mouth was sore and dry, and my stomach grumbled. Cody came back with a small cup of water. This was the same cup I had made on the ship. "It took this from the ship," he informed. I sipped the water. It quenched my thirst. I felt a little better after eating, but I was thirsty again, almost immediately.

Cody stayed and took care of me, as I rested. Even though I had been asleep for some time, I was still tired. The skin on my face was peeling because they had left me in the sun for some time while I was in my mini coma. My eyes hurt badly, and my body was sore as if I had been through another battle. It seemed every time I used my power, I was a little stronger, and healed a little quicker.

The problem was each time I had tried to do a little more than last time and I ended up more exhausted than the last time. I knew I needed to be alert, in case Ralph showed up, except I was sure I would be of no use if that happened. I had barely any strength to move, let alone, fight. I would need someone else to help if he came before I healed.

For two days, Cody went on caring for my needs. I rested. I got up a few times, but only a few. My legs trembled when I walked, so I would drop back onto the couch.

On the third day, I was up early. I jumped up off the couch with energy. I had slept like never before. Everyone was asleep. I walked towards the ladder and climbed down. I went out of the tree house. I climbed down its limbs to the bottom. My energy was back, and I was ready for an amazing day.

The sun shone into the rainforest. I sunk in the mud, almost immediately. Water soaked the ground, from the rain, the night before. I walked over to a blackberry bush. The blackberries were ripe. I ate the blackberries until the hunger faded. I walked over to the campfire.

I sat down on a log and ate the rest of my berries. Today, I could chew without exhaustion. My vision was better. Blackberries were a sweet treat.

I looked up, as I saw the sun flash in front of me. I scanned the sky. It was extraordinarily bright. It was as if the light was getting closer though. I stood up, as the light continued towards me getting larger and brighter by the moment. The light stopped and levitated in front of me. The light dropped to the ground, and I had to look away, or I felt it would burn my eyes.

Suddenly, the light was gone, and a young man stood in its place. He looked around eighteen. He had my same brown hair that went back with the same natural, wavy style. He had a bulky body, similar to Ralph but larger. His face was familiar. He wore a blue Quicksilver shirt with tan shorts that were too short. He wore black, Nike socks, up slightly above his bulky calves. He had to have been five to six years older than me. His face was intimidating. It looked as though he had been through many wars. He looked tough. His eyes had a shiny glare.

I spoke, "Titus?" I knew his name, but that was about it. "So, you know who I am?" he asked.

I stated, "I know your name, but not who you are."

"I am your brother," he informed.

"You are the one that told Ralph to kill me," I said.

He responded, "I did, but it was only a test. I wanted to know what would happen. I'm here now to see if you will be part of my cause. There is a price to pay for it, though."

I asked, "What cause? No first, who are we and how do we have powers? What are they, and who else has them?"

He responded, "My power is shape-shifting. I am like you. I can shapeshift and have the capabilities of the person I shift into. The Imperium Stone gave us power beyond any other. We are stronger than what the gods were. Ralph, Jack, Trent, they are nothing compared to us."

I blurted, "Trent?"

Titus responded, "Our other brother. He can make lightning. A year ago, I started a rebellion when the Meta's were together. That is what we call the beings with powers like us. All Metas trained at a facility on another world called mellontikos. It was there that the rebellion began and was fought. We rebelled, and we call ourselves The Tellus.

There are about a thousand of us. Technically, everyone has a power in the world, but there are about a thousand of us that have enhanced abilities. Humans have powers, they don't know about. Like, some can hold their breath for a long time, or some can lift incredible amounts of weight. Things that don't seem like powers but are."

Half of the entire Meta school joined me. Trent did not. A war started between the two sides. We were much more powerful, and the war didn't last long before they surrendered. We won, but we chose to establish a separate training facility on earth. We met as a council with the Metas and agreed to separate our people into the two groups, the Metas, and the Tellus.

We could have killed them, but we chose and came to earth. They have chosen to go on, abusing their powers, and are trying to stop us from improving the world. We want what is best for the world. We want to be able to help stop the suffering and violence. They benefit from it, so they are trying to block our attempts to help.

You decided that once you joined the school of Metas, you would go with whatever side Trent chose. We have other plans and need your help at our headquarters."

I responded, "That is a lot to process."

He responded, "I know, but you must understand this is critical to our survival. I've watched you and you have a pure heart. You are loyal, and we need another one of us if we are going to stop these Meta's."

I stated, "What loyalty, and what do you mean by we are more powerful than everyone else? I can control plants, which is cool, but I've been beaten almost daily."

He spoke, "Oh Azeal!"

"Wait, Azeal? Why did you call me Azeal?"

"Your real name is Azeal. When they wiped your memory, they programmed you with a new name."

"Anyway, if you think controlling plants is your strongest power, then you haven't even begun. There were three of us. Something so powerful that every Meta and all the gods teamed up and used their power to break it. It was as old as the heavens and was the power that formed the stars called the Imperium Stone. Three people got power from this stone. You, Davis Grant, who is our grandfather, and I received our power from The Emperium Stone."

"That's crazy," I responded.

"The Emperium Stone passed its powers to us and was destroyed, except for one fragment called Helios. The other Meta's got their power from the fragmented Helios stone. This is the same stone that gave the gods their powers, but I am not here to give you a history lesson."

I asked, "What is the price I must pay?"

Titus stated, "You need to kill Ralph. You chose, and killing your own brother is a lot to ask, but we need you more than him. He has a black heart and is a danger to everyone. He cannot be allowed to leave this island."

"I will pick you up when the job's done," he informed.

"Okay," I responded in, confusion.

Titus said, "Oh and George, I am sorry our crazy parents did this horrible thing to you."

"Did our parents strand me here?" I asked.

Titus responded, "Yes, but not really. Our father was tricked, and he was killed, trying to murder a great man fighting for our cause. Our father was evil. He thought he was doing the right thing, but he was not. He was a Meta. He controlled ice and could create it with his mind. He could shoot it out of his hands like Ralph with fire.

After he died, our mother remarried. She tried to rebuild but she was destroyed by the loss of our father. They both went crazy and were afraid of us. They put you here and erased your memory to hide you and your brothers from me. It took me a long time to find you."

"Who was the man that murdered our father?" I asked.

Titus went pale, "Once you murder Ralph, then all of your questions can be answered."

Titus started to make a formation in the air with his hand He was getting smaller by the second. He was soon a hummingbird. He was a beautiful glowing bird, unlike any I had ever seen, with purple, pink, red, and green. He was majestic. He suddenly darted from my view. "Wait!" I yelled, but he was gone.

I was shaking. He showed strength. He talked about being an all-powerful being, even compared to others with powers. I wondered what other powers I had. This was like every other situation. I got a few answers, and it only brought more questions.

I knew I could not kill my brother, but if I didn't, then Titus could easily come back and kill me. He knew his full strength, but I did not. I was in a pandora's box that within an answer were more questions. I would have to live like that unless I did what Titus said. I wanted to believe what Titus had said, but what he had said sounded wrong. He had tricked Ralph into a terrible cause, but I wouldn't follow unless I knew for sure. His cause sounded right, but he wanted me to kill my own brother. I hated Ralph for killing Jack, but he was still my brother.

I sat down at the fire-pit and contemplated the situation. He had told me so much, but I felt as if he told me nothing. I wanted to share what had happened, but no one was going to believe that I was more powerful than the gods and by the way, an all-powerful hummingbird told me.

I had done some horrible things. I wished Jack were alive. He could have helped with so much. Cody was the only one truly on my side. I could not put any more pressure on him.

Soon, everyone was up. Cody walked over. I was still sitting on the log, lost in thought. My head was drooping down. Cody walked over and sat on the log next to me. "What's up? Good to see that you're feeling better," he mentioned.

"Nothing much," I responded.

"Are you sure?" he asked.

"No, there are just a few things on my mind," I stated.

"What's that?" he asked.

"My brother," I responded.

He spoke, "What about Ralph?"

"Not Ralph," I answered.

"Jack?" he asked.

"No," I mentioned, "Titus. My oldest brother." I said

"How do you know you have an older brother?" he asked.

I spoke, "I have four older brothers. Titus visited me today. He told me to do something I don't want to do. I am scared not to."

"What did he ask you to do?" he posed.

"I can't tell you," I said.

"Okay, I understand. You're a good guy George and I'm sure you'll find an answer," he responded. He patted me on the shoulder and got up.

"I'm glad you are feeling better," he said as he turned to walk away. Soon, we were all having breakfast.

Usually, we only had dinner, but today was different. We all sat down at the fire pit. They roasted a pig and bananas in a deep sand pit. The bananas were yellow and looked ready to eat. The pig looked amazing. I was still very hungry, and we needed to get our strength back. The breakfast cheered me up, and everyone was being pleasant for once. "What is the special occasion?" I asked.

"Nothing," responded Chris.

Stacy spoke, "Are you okay today, like are you feeling better?"

I responded, "I am."

Stacy stated, "I think I speak for everyone. We are sorry we were being rude. We were all so excited to get home."

I informed, "No I should be the one apologizing. I was selfish on the boat."

Christopher interrupted, "Enough with the apologies. I am starving, let's eat." We ate and talked, and my worries left me. The food was delicious, and there was more than we needed. The bananas were smooth and creamy. Since I had been on this island, I had learned to eat less and less, so I would not have as much a problem with feeling hungry. Most of the time, it was still difficult.

Everyone went off swimming. I stayed behind. I was not in the mood, and Cody was not either. "What do you want to do?" Cody asked.

"I don't know," I responded. "Something totally off topic, but I liked to watch my sisters fencing matches," Cody stated.

I responded, "I know what I want to do."

Two limbs broke away from a nearby tree and started to fly towards us. The limbs transformed into my version of fencing swords as they landed at our feet. The swords had blunt ends but would be great for play. We both picked up our sword and faced each other. Cody spoke, "Oh okay. How is this going to work?"

I responded, "How about if you knock someone to the ground it's a point, and three hits to the body are equal to one point."

Cody asked, "How many points to win."

I responded, "How about three." I was soon in a battle stance. The sword felt perfect in my hand. I came at Cody with a strike to the chest. He parried with a downward block to my sword, then he spun to the right. I ran past him.

I darted at Cody and lunged at his shoulder. Cody swung his sword down at my leg. The sword hit my knee. He swept me off my feet and I dropped my sword. It crashed across the dirt as I fell to my back. The blow to the shin hurt, but not as much as when I hit the ground. I got a mouth full of dirt. I licked my teeth and realized they had dirt on them.

As I gulped, an unpleasant taste ran down my throat. Cody spun his sword. "One point for me," he said.

"I know, you are better than me," I stated.

"Get ready for a beating. I thought all this fighting would make you tougher, small one."

"Ha-ha! You're dead!"

Oh, I like the fire." Cody put his arm out, and he helped me up. I retrieved my sword and got in a battle stance. This time Cody came at me. He swung his sword at my shoulder. I parried. I swung my sword at him. When his sword clashed at mine, his shot through the air. It spun to the dirt. I slashed my sword at his shoulder. He remained still.

He darted towards his sword. As he bent down to regain his sword, I slashed at his back. He fell to the ground. His face hit first as he rolled to his back His face had dirt everywhere on it. He coughed up dirt. "Nice," he said.

"You are welcome," I responded. He regained his sword. He got back into a battle stance. "One, one," he spoke. I advanced towards Cody. He slashed at my head and I ducked but hit my shin again. He slashed at my leg again.

My left leg collapsed. I was on one leg. Rocks dug into my skin. The impact cut me, and when I shifted, it made the pain worse.

I blocked the strike, but he swung down at my shoulder. The sword made a huge *clang*. His sword flew.

His sword had not hit my shoulder. It had hit my shield. I had pulled my gray shield out at the last second. The shield glistened in the afternoon sun.

"You cheated," Cody stated.

"I know," I responded. Cody ran after his sword, but the sword shot off through the air. I could barely see the sword it was going so fast. Cody jumped out of the way, into the dirt again. The sword was now in my hand. I spoke, "You win."

Cody asked, "Why didn't you finish the match?"

I responded, "I saw your face. That hit to the shoulder would have hurt."

"Fair enough," Cody stated.

"I am still bragging about that to the others," Cody bragged.

"Okay," I responded. I threw the swords down to the ground, and I transformed my shield. I put the carving back in my pocket.

I felt a sudden surge of energy. I shot back, and my back hit the dirt. The back of my head smashed into a tree. I sat up and wiped the dirt from my back. The back of my head had bumps and bruises on it already. "What was that?" asked Cody.

"I do not know," I responded.

"You didn't trip. You like shot back," he stated.

I responded, "Yeah, I suddenly was just floating back to the ground. I felt my foot moving, but I didn't trip."

"What the heck," he spoke. I brought my shoe up to see what was on it. I inspected and saw immediately that had caused the problem. Seeds had sprung and wrapped around my shoes without my instruction. I stated, "It must be my power. I have not used it much and there is."

My sentence was cut off as I shot into the air. Leaves and branches smashed against me as I shot through the trees. I couldn't stop myself and the pain was almost unbearable. The wind blew in my face.

A stick ripped through my shirt and stabbed my shoulder. I stopped myself in the air, just as I cleared the trees. I got hurt a lot, but I never got used to it. Blood trickled onto my shirt, staining it. I had gashes on my face and arms. I could see but that did not help. I didn't want to pull the stick out of my shoulder but knew I couldn't leave it in. Pain was becoming a familiar theme and I had started not to mind it as much. The stick had to come out.

I turned my head away from the stick. It was long and as I forced it out, I heard a gruesome noise as the stick popped out of my shoulder. The pain was horrible. I tried to think of other things, but it was a deep hot pain. I had started to heal faster after each battle and could already feel my body repairing the damage. I rested for a minute.

I peered across the sky. All I could see below me were lush green leaves. It looked as if I could walk across the treetops as I could grass. The jungle was beautiful from overhead. (I should do this more often). The sky was overcast. I knew it would rain tonight. The sea had massive waves. I could see everything.

The mountain had its water splashing over the waterfall, and I could even see what was on the other side of that. The falls were the most beautiful area on the island. Rock formations and tropical plants lined that area. The granite rock of the mountain formed a cove there unlike any other on the island. I could even see the small shack from here. I saw the bright trees and the lush grass beneath the mountain. I gazed at my arms and legs. It was hard to put into perspective the last few months of my life, from not know who I was to fly.

I wanted to fly. I wanted to see how fast I could go and what the island was like. I wanted to see what was going on, and I wanted to speak to Ralph most of all. Working together would make us stronger and we would be able to leave the island easily. I wanted that, and I hoped he did too.

I summoned two seeds from the jungle floor. They shot up through the air and I grasped them in my hands. They were miniscule and dark brown. They erupted around my arms, and soon I had smooth wooden gloves. I felt more stable flying on both hands and feet. I could not resist the impulse to test my power.

I boosted off with no thought at all. I felt the rush of the wind shooting past me. The cool breeze felt great on my face. My hair flung back as I wove in and out between the mountains. I was flying at what seemed like an incredible speed. Even the thought of flying while I was flying seemed impossible. I had never thought of flying until a few days ago.

I jolted to a stop. I was levitating above the mountain and the waterfall. The flat mountaintop held terrible memories, but it was a beautiful place. Even the waterfall brought me a smile. Water shot over the edge and the pond had the clearest water I had ever seen. The granite rock glistened in the sun. The quaint shack was not too far away. It had no doors as our tree house did. The shack was tiny, and I couldn't imagine how seven people could sleep there. I felt terrible for them.

All the kids were outside except Ralph. Everyone's faces were red. Their eyes had lines under them. Their clothes were tattered and torn. The teenagers slumped and moaned in agony. "How long is he going to take?" Chloe bellowed.

Elijah hollered, "I hate this. He leaves to murder George and the others and leaves us here to suffer."

Marissa bellowed, "How could he do this to us. He is the strongest. We shouldn't be doing the heavy lifting."

Arthur corrected, "We are suffering, but he is doing this for us. He will enslave George, and then George will make us a mansion. We can't keep living this way."

"Shut up!" Elijah yelled.

Marissa argued, "Yeah Arthur, why do you always have to see the bright side in things."

"Yeah Arthur," Elijah blurted.

Marissa muttered, "You realize Ralph uses us like slaves. He is all like, do this, do that. It sucks. I don't even know if he is telling the truth half of the time."

Arthur grumbled, "He is still doing it for the better."

"Idiot," Elijah mumbled. Elijah walked over towards Arthur. His fists clenched. I shot to the ground.

"Stop!" I yelled. Everyone winced as I landed with a crash that cracked the rocks beneath us.

"Don't hurt us," Marissa said.

"I won't," I responded.

"Why are you here?" Arthur asked.

I responded, "I was curious about what was going on, but this is worse than I imagined."

Elijah stated, "Uh you mean how he's going to murder those people down there, dawg."

"Is that true?" I asked.

"Yes," Marissa responded.

"When did he leave?" I asked."

"Two hours ago," Arthur added

"I have to go, but I'll be back soon," I said

Chloe asked, "Can I go with you?"

"Sorry, there's no time," I informed. I closed my eyes, and relaxed. I thought of Ralph. He would murder the people that had helped me out. He had done this to Jack, and I could not let this happened again.

"Are you going to do anything?" asked Arthur.

"Yes," I responded.

I opened my eyes and shot off the granite mountain top like a burst of light. My flight fell silent as I broke the sound barrier streaking across the treetops back to Cody and the others. I noticed my injuries had already healed. I was getting stronger.

I jolted to a stop and dropped to the ground. I landed on the spot where I was standing with Cody. Cody was still there "Where did you go?" he asked.

"Not enough time," I stated.

"What's up?" he asked, "You take off, and come back without telling me where you went, and now you are ignoring me."

I responded, "Yeah, because Ralph will murder everyone if we don't help."

"Oh gosh," Cody said. We darted through the rainforest. This couldn't happen again, and I was determined to stop him. I swatted the plants out of my way. I heard Cody running behind me. I heard the water.

We moved through the forest quickly and soon we were at the pond. The water was blood red. The body of Chris floated at the top. He was sprawled out and floating lifeless. He had a huge wound in his chest that was still bleeding.

The bodies of our friends lay twisted on the ground, spread across the beach. Their shirts were ripped, and they had holes in most of their chests. They had clearly been caught by surprise. "Oh gosh," Cody spoke as he sobbed. Tears rolled down my cheeks. I fell on my knees. I held my hands over my mouth. I was too sad to be angry. I forgot about the danger as I felt the shame and pain of losing my friends.

I remembered the words in my dream that Jack spoke. "You failed us." This went through my head over and over. I was heartbroken. I had truly failed everyone.

I heard a Chuckle. I heard Cody scream, "Ralph," then he fell to the ground. I felt something hit my back. The blow was excruciating. I fell face down in the dirt. I was sick of all the blood and dirt that came with this island and I was ready to make it stop.

"*WHAT HAVE YOU DONE*?" I demanded.

Ralph walked in front of me. "I'm going home," he stated.

I responded, "Titus asked me to do the same thing. He is a madman. He told you and I to murder each other."

He stated, "No, he came to you because he wanted to trick you. He told me he would."

I asked, "Why are you telling me this?"

He responded, "Because you won't live long enough to tattle-tale."

"Why did he not just kill me where I stood?" I asked.

He stated, "He told me that you are prophesied to kill him when he is at the peak of his power. If I kill you now when you don't know your full strength, then he will take me home as a reward."

I argued, "But what is there to gain?"

"Everything," he responded. I was still on my knees. Ralph swung at my face. I caught his punch in my hand. Ralph didn't expect that and came back with a blow to the face with his other hand. The punch was a glancing blow, but it still hurt. He was strong, and he was much better of a fighter than me. My eye felt destroyed. I had trouble seeing for a minute.

"Please don't do this?" I pleaded.

He spoke, "You think I feel compassion for you. Do you not see I've murdered all of your friends, including Jack?" Ralph kneed me in the face. My head whipped back. "Get up," Ralph ordered.

"I can't," I responded.

"How dare you," he spoke as he swung at my gut. This shot knocked the wind out of me. I fell to my side. I tried to breathe, but I couldn't. I rolled over to see Ralph holding Cody by the neck.

"Enough!" he yelled

He had hit me hard, but I could already feel myself healing. Strength surged through me. I acted as if it took some effort to stand. Cody looked at me in shock as Ralph ordered us to start walking. He walked behind Cody with a spot of fire floating behind Cody's head in case we tried to resist. Ralph laughed, "I have a lot of work for you before I can let you die!"

Chapter Sixteen

My mind raced as we made the long walk back to the top of the mountain. Ralph didn't know that I was there only moments ago. Cody was exhausted, and he was severely injured. I would act like I needed a break to allow Cody, to rest and Ralph would beat me.

Ralph was full of rage. His fists were giant, and his blows to my face were hard and accurate. I was a mess by the end of the walk. My eyes had bruises all over them and I could barely see. Each time he beat me, I could feel the healing start immediately.

I couldn't help but notice how beautiful the rainforest was. Calluna bushes were all around the forest. Tropical plants were everywhere, and the trees provided shade.

We were walking a different way. We moved through swamps and marshes. It drenched our clothes and we were covered in mud. The sun dried the mud on us, so it stuck and then we would wade back into the mud like quicksand. This would make Ralph angry and he would beat me again.

Finally, the mountain was right ahead of us. It was massive. Even with everything that we faced we were happy that we were done hiking. Cody flashed me a worried look. I had to find a way to get Cody away from Ralph, so I could stop him and save the others. I couldn't allow him to kill any more of my friends. I had to come up with a plan soon or he was going to beat me to death.

It took about a half hour to complete the hike up the mountain. Cody needed help and Ralph made me carry him the last part of the hike. We finally made it to the top.

I saw the clear water flowing down the waterfall. This only brought back bad memories. I saw the shack again, where they lived. I wanted to burn it down. "The prodigal son is home," Elijah beamed. Ralph pushed me to the ground. I fell to my knees. "What took you so long?" asked Chloe.

"Don't trifle with me," Ralph ordered.

"Okay," responded Chloe.

"Where is my food?" asked Ralph.

"You didn't ask for food," argued Arthur.

"Get me some," demanded Ralph.

Arthur argued, "We have been working all day."

"Do as I say," Ralph commanded. This conversation went on with Ralph demanding every little thing. Ralph took Cody with him and they left me to sleep on the granite floor in the shack, so I could rest because Ralph said I would need my energy. I didn't know why he hadn't killed me yet. I lay down for hours it seemed.

He woke me up with a punch to the face. My face had healed some but each time he hit me it hurt like the first time. My eye was bruised again and swollen. I jumped up. Ralphs' face was grim. "You ready to get to work?" he asked.

I nodded, wanting to punch him in the gut.

"Come with me," he ordered.

I walked behind Ralph outside the shack. Once we were outside, he stated, "You are going to build me a headquarters on this mountain-top."

"What?" I asked.

"You heard me."

"No."

"I was very generous with the nap. Do it or else Cody dies. I can do it in a second." I had to do what he said for now. I closed my eyes.

"Do you always have to close your eyes like that?" he asked.

I responded, "I have to concentrate, closing my eyes helps."

"Okay, go on," he ordered. I closed my eyes again. I concentrated my power. I tried to search with my mind to detect where the living organisms in the seeds were. Soon, I opened my eyes. I saw thousands of seeds shooting towards us through the air. They shot right past us to a large open area next to the river. They all jolted to a stop. Seeing them all levitate was still amazing. I held them in the air for a moment and then split them into three lanes. Then I moved, all three sides to different points. "How long is this going to take you?" asked Ralph.

"Wait," I responded. The seeds grew. They became thick, long trunks. They stacked on each other. Lifting the trunks was mentally a challenge. The trees stuck together making thick walls. Soon, the walls were tens of feet high. The roof was now forming. I soon imagined the inside. I imagined what it might look like. Trunks floated through the doorway.

This went on for over an hour. More seeds and more walls. Ralph constantly demanding more rooms and larger training areas. I was at the edge of my power and finally trembling I fell to the ground. I had used up most of my energy.

"So, it is good?" Ralph asked.

I responded, "It should be."

The mansion was gargantuan. It was three stories high and stretched around and up most of the hillside. Ralph and the others shoved me out of the way to go inside. I slowly got up and walked towards the doorway.
I walked through the doorway to a massive entry hall. Imagining what could be in here was nothing like seeing it. I walked into a large living room with many couches and a fire pit. A large hole was in the ceiling to let the smoke out. Rooms stretched out to both sides down long corridors of the building. At the back were a variety of training and meeting rooms.
The bedrooms were in the south wing of the building. The bedrooms were large with dressers and large beds. All the bedrooms were the same. There were stairs to the second story. I walked into an open room with nothing in it. To my left was a room with cabinets and an island. To my right was a large, open room with a climbing wall on each wall. That was the most strenuous part of the design process.

Everyone had taken off their shoes and started climbing. Suddenly Ralph stepped into the room and ordered everyone out.

"Boy, come over here."

I did as he said. Cody was still locked away somewhere I couldn't find.

"At the entrance I want you to make a logo that says, "Ralph's Palace!", then below it should say Praise Ralph."

I responded, "Who do you think you are? You're not a king."

"Do as I say," Ralph bellowed.

"Okay," I responded.

I walked down step by step to the bottom story. I walked outside to the front overhang at the entrance. I thought of doing what Ralph asked, but I rebelled. I wrote **Ralph Sucks**, then I walked back inside. My face had already mostly healed, and I was less and less concerned about his beatings.

I walked up the stairs towards Ralph. Ralph had his arms folded. He was gazing at the climbing wall.

"What would you have me do my lord?"

"Don't call me that," he responded.

"Okay," I said. Ralph ordered me to get back to work. For the next two days he demanded I do a variety of different things for him. I either had to go hunt animals for food and blankets or I was building. Every task seemed to get harder. It eventually rained, and I was sopping wet. Ralph still demanded that I work. Sweat mixed in with the water that dripped onto my clothes. I felt the clothes sticking to me and I was miserable.

Ralph eventually found out what I had done at the entryway and he gave me the worst beating yet. It was worth it, and I was right back off to work after that.

He made me convert the shack into one humongous master suite. That was going to be his room. His bed was king sized. It had all these unique features he wanted. On the back and side of the poles of the bed, it was engraved with *Ralph almighty*. He had a dresser for no reason. He had a couch on the side of the room. It had comfy arms rests and was the perfect height for Ralph. There was a large counter on the other side of the couch with built in storage. He was the only one that received the animal skins to make warm blankets and clothes. He was very pleased with his room, and that day was when he was the nicest to me.

At day's end, I was spent. I had built stairways up the mountain and lookouts with railings and defense positions as if they were to fight a war. I had not rested, and I could barely walk. I passed out many times when I was working.

They had not fed me much since we got here. I was worried about Cody. I hadn't seen him since we got there. I needed to find him and come up with a plan to free all of us. It was dark, and I was in Ralph's room asking him what my next task would be.

"Go rest," he responded.

"Are you serious?" I asked.

"You've had a long day," he stated.

" Okay," I said.

I walked away quickly and found the small room they locked me in at night and laid down. I sprawled out across the cold floor. No storm could have stopped me from falling asleep, and soon I did.

I woke up to the sound of my door opening and footsteps. I still wanted to sleep and slowly opened my eyes. I focused just in time to see a boot coming hard at my face. In the same instant I got hit in the shoulder with something so hard that I shot through the wall of my room and out onto the Granite mountain-top. My shoulder had a gaping hole in it and was bleeding profusely. I tumbled across the granite but before I could stop, I was hit hard again by another bolt that sent me tumbling over a ledge. Everything went black. I opened my eyes. My ears were ringing, and my shoulder and leg felt like they had been crushed. I couldn't move.

I looked around and found I was on the edge of the waterfall. Ralph had me in his tight muscular grip hanging from my wounded leg, upside down over the edge of the waterfall. It was early morning and was barely light out. The clear water was soaking my clothes. I never guessed this was his plan. I thought I would have time to come up with a plan.

My wounds were so painful I was in and out of consciousness. I shook and was sure that I was in shock. I looked below and found I was hundreds of feet in the air. I had imagined how far the drop was but knowing I could fall was outrageous. That would be fatal on a good day. I didn't think I'd survive. Even if I had a chance of surviving, I would still be knocked out, and I would drown.

"No Ralph," I asked.

"Shut up?" he yelled.

I responded, "I tended your every need. Can you fake my death? Please, Ralph. You can't kill a brother."

He laughed, "I have done it once. It ain't that hard. I have everything to gain from Titus. He is always watching. Somehow."

I stated, "Maybe we can take him down together."

Ralph shook his head, then said, "That is not possible. Titus could kill us with the blink of an eye."

I spoke, "You are right."

Ralph asked, "What did you say?"

I responded, "You are right. You have everything to gain. You don't need me."

Ralph stated, "Okay then, let's do this."

Ralph grabbed my shoulder with his other hand and whispered into my ear as he had with Jack, "Have a fun ride."

A split second before Ralph released me, I clicked the button on my carving. My shield developed, and I swung at Ralph. The gray shield clashed against his chin. He fell back. He fell right into the water with a huge splash. I dropped into the water and almost lost consciousness again. My shoulder and leg were still bleeding. Water splashed onto my face and brought me back to reality.

"Oow!" Ralph murmured.

I tried to get to my knees and faced him. My shoulder wouldn't work and as I looked up, he kneed me in the face. I tasted blood again and the ringing was back in my ears. He had knocked me back into the water and I was drowning and unable to climb out. He left me there for a minute and then reached in and grabbed me by the throat. I was off my feet and he held me with one hand. It grasped his arm. I jerked and turned every which way. Ralph was too strong.

Ralph took a step towards the edge of the waterfall. I accepted my fate. I had failed everyone, and Titus and Ralph had succeeded. Tears ran down my cheeks as blackness formed in the corner of my eyes. I felt myself go limp in his grasp. He held me like a lifeless carcass after a hunt.

I felt him relax his grasp around my neck, then I was falling. I waved my arms. Water splashed on me. I plummeted. I was falling and tumbling faster and faster. I saw the beautiful granite rock.

A gargantuan lake was below me. The water was clear, and sand curled around the lake. The half circular granite wall enclosed half of the lake. Tropical plants on this side were the only plants I could see. The granite below the lake made the reflections turn to rainbows.

Many small waterfalls fell from the granite mountain toppled into the lake. This view was amazing. I felt no control. I fell hundreds of feet as I spun through the air. I tried to focus and call seeds from the shore, but my mind was too blurry from the pain. I knew this was the end. I saw the water rushing up at me and closed my eyes and thought one last time about a seed. The water smashed into my side first like a giant sledge hammer. I blacked out.

Chapter Seventeen

I felt a thump against my chest and then another and another. I was foggy, and I kept feeling pressure. It was as if I was choking or coughing. I opened my eyes. Water shot out of my mouth. I started coughing and sputtering. More water poured out onto the granite I was laying on. I was on the shiny granite that I had seen earlier from above. I gagged and took deep breaths.

I looked up to see the sun shining down on a figure standing over me. All I could think was Ralph. The sun shone too brightly on my eyes. The figure was only a silhouette. I stopped struggling and lay silent on the granite. I had no strength and my injuries still burned in my leg and shoulder. My head felt bruised and I felt nauseous. The rock didn't feel great on my bruises. I could barely see. This truly was at an all-time low.

The figure spoke in a familiar voice.

"Oh my gosh. He did it to you too."

I could barely speak, but I asked in a very scratchy voice, "Who are you?"

He offered, "Let me help you up." His hand reached out, and I grabbed it. He seemed strong like Ralph. As someone lifted me, my bruises hurt more. I shook as I tried to stand.

I looked at the figure for a second and tried to focus. My eyes cleared, and my heart stopped. I recognized this face but couldn't believe it. He had his sea-blue eyes and his blond surfer hair glistened the same way. He was bulkier, but I recognized him.

"This is not possible," I exclaimed.

He responded, "I know, but I'm here, and you survived." He flipped his blond surfer hair to the side. His clothes were soaked.

"What happened?" Jack asked.

"I have that same question for you," I responded.

"How, how, how did you? How did you save me?"

"I was swimming in the lake when I saw something drop. I didn't think it was a person, so I ignored it. I continued to swim. After a minute I swam to the bottom of the lake. Did I mention I can hold my breath for, I don't even know how long? I can sleep in the water."

I blurted, "Okay stay on track. What happened when you swam to the bottom?"

Jack answered, "When I dove down, I saw you laying there lifeless. Your mouth was open. I was instantly confused and terrified. So, I brought you up and tried to bring you back."

"How did you survive without us? I'm so sorry." I said

"Let's talk in my hut," he ordered. I was starting to heal but he still had to pick me up and carry me through the rainforest. Palm trees shaded us. He had picked a beautiful area with lush green grass. Smooth and silky leaves brushed against my arms. There were flower beds and coconuts hanging from the trees. Jack was more built now. He walked with pride.

Soon, we came to large cone-shaped hut. It had mud on the outside that molded the wood together. It was large, but still not big enough for two of us to sleep in. There were two logs near the hut.
I sat on one, and Jack sat on the other. The wood was smooth, and Jack had chipped the bark off the logs.

Jack clasped his hand, "Well I guess I should start. The last time you saw me I was plummeting to my death."

"Yeah."

"Well anyway, what you didn't see was that I plummeted in terror. I closed my eyes ready for death. Then, I jolted to a stop and was fine. I had no cuts, no bruises and no pain. I opened my eyes and found that the water had caught me before I hit the bottom. Water really is a part of me. Ever since then I have lived here. My power has grown and grown and now I can do things I could never have fathomed. I have had some of the loneliest days ever. It is so great to have you here."

I asked, "Why didn't you come back?"

"As time passed, everything scared me. I didn't know if you were even alive. I was lonely, but Ralph frightened me too much, so I just stayed here."

"You were right to stay here," I said in shame.

"Why?"

"Because I screwed up. I learned what my power was and started to learn how to use it. I was immediately faced with battle after battle that almost killed me. I even met our brother Titus. Just when I had finally learned to not use my power to help and not for only my own amusement, I decided to leave for just a minute and it had horrible consequences.

"What happened?"

I said slowly, "He killed them. Almost all of them. Cody is alive, I think. Ralph used his powers and burnt holes through their chests. He left them dead on the ground for me to see. He let their blood stain the pond. He showed he'd do anything to get home."

I sobbed. Tears rolled down my cheeks like heavy rain. Tears built up on my lip.

"You did your best," Jack comforted.

I stuttered, "No I didn't. I used the gift only for my benefit and a lot of people were killed."

"You think you're the only person who messed up. I did nothing. I stayed here afraid while you were helping as much as you could. If anyone is a failure, then it is me."

"Thanks," I said.

Jack asked, "You said something about our brother."

"Titus," I said.

"Who?"

I responded, "Our brother Titus Grant. He has powers like me and you, but stronger. I mean he is so much stronger. He can shape-shift into whatever he wants. He flew down like a beam of light and left as a hummingbird. He transformed into his regular state when we talked.

He told me how we got to the island, and why. He told me I had **Meta** abilities like you guys, but he said my powers now were nothing compared to what they will be...."

I told him every detail there was of what Titus had said. By the time I stopped, I was very weak. My wounds were sapping my energy as my body tried to heal. We were still sitting on the logs outside his hut.

"What is the plan," he asked.

I responded, "I am starving."

"Raw fish?" he asked.

"I haven't ever eaten any, but sure."

He darted off down the trail, and I heard a splash in the water. He was back in moments. He prepared them, and we ate the delicious fish, raw. I needed to eat to help with the healing process. I felt like at least one thing in my world was right being able to be with Jack.

After dinner, we continued to talk.

Jack asked, "So I must ask. How did Ralph beat you this time?"

I responded, "Oh you start out with a sucker-punch to the throat. I forgot how rude you were."

We both laughed.

I spoke, "He took Cody hostage and forced me to work or he would kill him. He beat the crap out of me over and over again for everything and nothing. He made me build all sorts of things for him. He said he wanted a place he could return to that would be a fortress for him. I built him a huge facility on the mountain side that had to have everything revolving around him. The constructs were so big they strained me to the core of my energy. He took up entire days having me do useless chores. Last night Ralph told me to go to sleep, then in the morning, I woke up to a kick to the face and he shot fireballs through my shoulder and leg so I couldn't move. I fought back, but he took about two seconds to beat me. I guess he was done with me and ready to get off the island."

"What would you do if you killed Ralph?"

"I wouldn't."

"Just if you did, what would you do?"

I responded, "What do you mean by that?"

Jack asked, "Well you heard what Titus told Ralph. It's the truth. It all makes sense. If Ralph kills you, it will be much easier for Titus. Titus is afraid of you, and that's a good thing. If you have more power, then you need to know what your powers are, but you don't."

"How does it make sense?"

"If Titus knows you are destined to kill him then it makes sense that he would ask Ralph to murder you. He told Ralph to murder you for his benefit."

I argued, "Why would Titus have come then?"

Jack's face lit up, "He saw that you were learning your power. He saw that Ralph wasn't going to go and kill you on his own. He needed you to fight him again, so Ralph could kill you. He knew even the minor ability you have now is powerful and if Ralph waited any longer, then you would survive. He needed you to be pushed towards stopping him, so he could kill you."

"Well then, why didn't he kill me where I stood?"

Jack responded, "He is afraid. He does not know how powerful he is. He doesn't want to fight another, what did you call it? Perium Meta. He needs someone else to do the dirty work for him."

I thought, then spoke, "I don't know what I would do. He scares me. I hope it doesn't get to that point."

"You have me. I will have your back if it goes that bad."

"Thanks, man," I said. Birds squawked. Trees swayed, and my hair blew in the breeze. The afternoon air was cool, and I was starting to get cold.

"Have you thought about Ralph any? Fighting him? Not for Titus's cause, but just to stop him?"

"No," I responded.

"I have. I know it is wrong, but even just getting the rest of the people out of there. Who knows, he could throw Cody down the waterfall any day. He's human, so the drop would kill."

"What did you do to pass time here?" I asked.

"You know, the usual. Swimming with the fish, and controlling the water to go up the waterfall, instead of going down it. Using water to help fly. How about you?"

"Same. Normal days, fighting a Sphinx and magical creatures. Making whatever the heck I want out of plants." We both laughed.

"Man, all the times I needed you to help me, It would have been so much easier. When I broke the ship, you could have controlled the water instead of me blacking out."

"Yeah, it is so great to have someone to rely on." We talked for what seemed like hours. We went through every single detail of what had happened. It was great to have Jack by my side. We laughed and told our stories. I had missed Jack so much. I had mourned over him and now it seemed all my worries were gone.

Titus, Ralph and all the horrid things in my life were shoved out of my brain. I was just there having a great time. When we were tired of sitting, Jack asked if I wanted to go see the fresh water where it meets the sea water.

"Sure."

Jack said, "Follow me."

We walked over to the lake. The clear freshwater stretched into a stream. The pond was lined with granite pebbles. The stream had a rocky bank and I kicked and skipped the rocks as we walked. The trees swayed. The beautiful purple and white tropical lignum vitae flowers were in full bloom all around the stream. Somehow, I had decided that in my previous life I knew a lot about plants.

As we walked, I asked, "So why are we going to see this place in particular?"

"It is cool how the two different colored waters, divide, then collide. I also want to show you how much cooler my power is than yours."

"Oh, so it is a competition now, is it?" I said, "Then if so, I would have already beaten you by now."

Jack said, "Okay, better hold your dukes up George, because this ain't gonna be pretty." I mocked, "Oh get cocky, and see where that gets you." Honestly, the hole in my shoulder and leg had closed but were still incredibly painful.

"Let's wait until we get there."

We continued to walk. It seemed like we had walked a couple miles and my body was feeling it. I was quiet as we walked.

I started panting, Jack asked, "What, you getting tired?"
"I am fine. You trying to get on my nerves? You know I was recently thrown off a waterfall."

Palm trees swayed, and the wind blew my hair to the side. We walked near some sharp palm trees right as we came into view of the ocean. "There it is," Jack stated.

"It's beautiful."

The sea water was dark blue. Rocks of all colors and textures were on the seashore. The river water met the ocean water in a perfect line. The waters did not collide but stayed separate as they were. The fresh water was clear though. It looked amazing. An island was close by that was comprised of steep mountains and cliffs. It was green and lush there. The water was dead calm where they met. The waters that divided almost looked unnatural. It was exquisite to look at.

Jack jumped high into the air and dove into the water; His jump made a huge splash. Jack shot under the water, fully submerged.

He started his demonstration and immediately water shot into the air about ten feet. The water spun into a huge circle. This circle was like a donut with another open circle in the middle. Then, a tornado of water shot up at least twenty feet in a thinner circle, inside the larger circle.

The water was clear and fresh. I had never seen anything so beautiful.

Jack sprouted out of the middle of the spinning tornado of water. He grinned, with a sparkle in his eye. He put his arms out.

"Can you do this?"

I responded, "No, I can do it better."

I closed my eyes. I concentrated my power. My mind raced. I imagined what I wanted. Two seeds shot under my feet. I shook. Then, I levitated above the ground. I flew straight up into the air. I flew up about 20 feet and then froze. I reached my arms out towards the rainforest. "Is that all you got?" he asked.

"You haven't seen nothing yet," I responded.

I had to imagine exactly what I wanted. I tried and waited but nothing happened.

"Oh, are your powers not working. It must disappoint you," Jack joked.

"Shut up. Wait until you see this."

I relaxed and concentrated. My eyes opened. Large palm trees shot into the air. I clenched my fists and as I did this the palm tree shattered into small stone like pebbles.

I pulled fruit out of nearby trees and they joined the stones as they shot towards Jack. Jack screamed as the mass of fruit and stones shot towards him.

Jack lost concentration and the water started to splash to the ground. His smile left, and his sparkling eyes showed fear. He stared at me. As the water dropped, he dropped. He flailed his arms out of control as he hit the water. It was all over in an instant. Jack stood up and looked at me. The fruit and stones were frozen in mid-air. It was amazing, like time had stopped.

I looked at Jack, "Was my thing too frightening for you?"

"Whatever," He mocked.

"Oh, poor baby. Do you need a shoulder to cry on?"

"Shut up." Jack stroked his hands through his hair, pushing it back. He stomped out of the water. Jack sat down on the sand, soaked. His face was red. He whipped his hair to the side. I took a step toward him, and everything fell to the ground.

"What did I do?" I asked.

"That was terrifying. I haven't been that scared since Ralph."

"I didn't mean to. I was just showing you something cool."

"Okay, sorry for getting mad."

I spoke, "Yeah all this caused was arguing. Let's eat some of this fruit.   "

He smiled, and we laid back and ate in the afternoon sun.

Chapter Eighteen

Later that afternoon, we walked back, soaked and tired, to the lake. I was always tired after using my powers. Sweat dripped down my neck. We had been running around in the sand and gotten wet of and on during the day and we were both wet and sticky for the walk back. The hike back was through bushes and muddy marsh areas which got us even dirtier. Both of us were spent from the walk by the time we got back.

Soon, we heard the waterfall. The clear water splashed down into the lake. Mist spread through the air. We were near the lake. I dropped to the ground. I sprawled out across the granite. My eyes closed, ready to go to sleep. Jack dropped to the ground, nearby me.

We started to talk about what we would do from here. The others would need help but now we could come up with a plan to save them all together. Suddenly, I heard a noise in the distance. I looked up.

Ralph was at the top of the waterfall. He held Cody, who was struggling to get out of Ralph's arms. Ralph leaned over the edge of the waterfall with Cody screaming, trying to get away. Ralph stepped calmly off the edge of the waterfall and hovered in midair.

Jack had his eyes closed and was still talking.

I kicked him lightly with my foot and said, "Look Up."

I pointed at Ralph holding Cody. By now Ralph had let go of the Cody. Ralph spread out his arms and legs. His entire body lit on fire. Cody continued to drop. Ralph's body was a menacing fiery figure. I spoke, "I'll get Cody you get," but Jack was already gone. He was darting across the water riding at top speed in a column of water 10 feet above the lake. Ralph was watching from above. He was hovering in place in the air waiting and watching hoping to see the impact.

Jack jumped up in the air. Water shot at his legs, which boosted him up higher and higher. He came at Cody from the side, and he wrapped his arms around him. They fell and splashed into the water.

"No!" Ralph bellowed.

I pulled in seeds and flew into the air.

"What, did you realize we are stronger than you thought?" Jack yelled at Ralph.

"You should be dead," he hollered.

Ralph shot towards me. His body looked like a missile on fire. He wore an evil grin. I jumped to the side just as he slammed into the ground where I was just standing.

"How?" He screamed

I responded, "Looks like Titus won't be visiting you soon."

"You won't be alive much longer."

His flame disappeared as he lunged at me and grabbed my neck.

He picked me up as I kicked and twisted trying to get away. I grabbed his arm trying to break his grip. I tried to punch him, but it did nothing. He was strong and much bigger than me.

The next thing I knew I fell to the ground. Ralph let go of me. I hit the granite on my right side. Jack was standing near me. He held out his hand to me. I grabbed it and he helped me up. Ralph lay on the ground.

Ralph got up as I did. "Typical Jack. George has to get his brother to save him."

"Why don't you shut up Ralph. You selfish jerk," mocked Jack.

Ralph ignited into flames. The heat from his flame was warm even from a distance. It felt nice. He levitated.

His voice had changed with the fire." Come up any time and I will kill both of you. If you don't, then I will come down and find you. George, you and I are going to end this."

Ralph shot off upwards towards the mountain. Cody hugged both of us.

"How did both of you survive?"

"That might have to wait."

"Why?" Jack asked.

I responded, "I'm going to stop him."

"Why?" Cody asked.

"If I kill him, then Titus will come, and I can deal with him. He is evil. I need to kill him or stop him, and I believe I am the only one that can."

"Makes no sense," Cody spoke.

"What about me?" asked Jack.

I responded, "Jack, I am tired of you having to save me. I have to do this on my own."

"Okay," he said

A seed shot into my hand. I balled it up, then I shook. I levitated. I rose above the ground. I skyrocketed up faster than I had ever flown before. The wind blew against me. My arms reached out to feel the granite rock as I felt the water rushing down the waterfall.

I stopped at the edge of the waterfall and dropped into the water. I trudged through the water and straight up to the doorway. The entry door opened, and Chloe walked over.

"George!" she exclaimed.

"Where's Ralph?" I asked.

"You shouldn't be here. Ralph will kill you."

"Chloe, what's up," Ralph walked into the room.

"Chloe duck," I yelled.

Chloe dropped to the ground. The seed shot out of my hand. The seed wrapped around her waist, and she shot past me and outside to safety.

I closed my eyes. I concentrated my power. Power surged through me. I opened my eyes. The couch shot up off the ground, then it shot through the air toward Ralph. The wooden couch punctured a pillar and shot right through it. The pillar broke in half. The ceiling drooped. The couch knocked Ralph off his feet. He hit his back against the floor.

"How does that feel," I mocked.

Ralph got up slowly. He grabbed the couch by the bottom and lifted it up. His hands shot beams of fire at the couch. The fire levitated the couch. The couch ignited in flames.

He shot the couch towards me. I closed my eyes and concentrated my power on the couch. It froze in mid-air. Ralph was controlling the fire that shot the couch toward me. I used my power to push against his power. The couch sat in between us, crumpling under the pressure and heat. He gave up, and so did I. The couch dropped to the floor.

Fighting Ralph inside wasn't an option. He was going to burn the building and everyone in it to the ground. It was already on fire.

"What are you going to do?" she asked from outside. The seed I had used for Choe came to my hand. I imagined what I wanted. The seed shot towards Ralph. A thick, wooden, donut shape formed around his neck. It ripped him towards the wall.

"Get out of here," I told Chloe.

The smoke was thick, and I was coughing. Flames were everywhere, and it was almost unbearable. I couldn't get up the stairs, but I had to get to the kids that were upstairs. I couldn't get to them, but I couldn't let them die. I could hear Ralph burning through his wooden collar inside the wall. I didn't have much time.

I knew what I had to do. A piece of wood came into my hand. I balled it up, then I shot out the door. I flew up to the roof of the mansion. I dropped towards the roof as I opened a hole, so I could pass through to the inside. I landed in the rock-climbing room. Arthur and Elijah lay on the ground. They had blacked out. It was much hotter up here, which made sweat drop from my face like raindrops. I could barely see, because it was so black. I could taste the ashes in my mouth and the heat felt like it would peel my skin. I grabbed both Arthur and Elijah and I shot up and out of the hole. I lowered to the ground near the water and tried to cool them. They lay looking lifeless.

"Stay here and breathe," I instructed.

I sighed, then I realized Marissa was still inside. I turned back towards the mansion. I could hear Ralph was free inside the mansion. There was a giant explosion and the whole front of the building blew apart and flew at us in a million pieces. Balls of fire shot around, and wood shot towards me. I used my power to stop the wood from hitting Elijah, Arthur or Chloe.

Ralph stood there in the fire facing us.

"It really is too bad. I thought Marissa was nice. Now she has blacked out by fire and died by explosion. Sad you did this to her," Ralph mocked

"You did this. You selfish sociopath. You're retarded. How could you do such a thing?"

"If you had left me alone, then she would be fine. If you had let me kill you the first time, then everyone you know would not be dead, so it is really your fault."

I dashed towards Ralph. Ralph flew up into the air about 50 feet. He ignited his entire body.

Next, I did something extraordinary I had never done before. I shot sideways in a flip away from Ralph and half way through the flip, I pressed the button on my carving. The shield transformed, and I launched it through the air towards Ralph. The shield shot like a rocket towards Ralph and knocked him into the side of the mountain. He slumped and rolled to the ground. He hit the granite slab below like a dead fish. I was starting to trust my strength.

I focused, and a seed shot towards Ralph. As it flew, it turned into a spike the size of my foot. It caught Ralph before he had time to get up and went right through his leg. Blood spilled out of his thigh.

"You!" he screamed in pain. I drug the spike like a chain and shot him towards a tree. He skidded across the granite. He bounced and spun, smashing his arms, legs and face against the rock. He slammed his back against the tree next to the old shack. Ralph was a mess.

As Ralph laid in a lump trying to burn the spike, Jack was zooming back and forth as he rode the water above me. He looked graceful as he glided across the water.

"Need my help now?" he asked.

"I would say no, but yeah. I need you to bring them down to Cody."

"Who?" Jack responded.

I answered, "Who do you think. Do you want to bring Ralph down there? Do something."

"Okay snappy," he answered as he shot over to the edge of the pond.

Jack picked both Arthur and Chloe up over his shoulders and rose through the air down the waterfall as I turned back to face Ralph. Ralph had burnt the spike and was starting to recover. His left hand lit on fire. Ralph shot a humongous pillar of fire towards me.

As I ran, the fire formed bars all around me. I looked around, but there was no hole large enough to escape through. This felt like I was some chicken in a microwave. Sweat dripped off my face. He walked towards me with a smug face. Ralph held onto the bars. He beamed, "Wouldn't you agree I am on fire with this whole capture thing. I mean I am totally crushing the competition." As he said this, I noticed the bars around me, starting to shrink. My space in here was getting smaller. Now I felt like a candle with a blowtorch right on me. My eyes closed, to shield from the brightness and heat. My time here was limited. I felt my skin peeling and re-growing at the same time.

I didn't know what me was around, so I ran. (Yep), right through the fire, as painful as it was. My clothes caught fire and it burned me severely as I passed through the bars. I ran to the water and dove in. Even with the heat, my body could repair. I could see clearer now. My senses were back.

I came out of the water onto a ledge. I looked down over the jungle. A tree shot towards me and shot right through the ground causing a large crack in the rock. Ralph shot towards me, still on fire. Grass rose and shot towards me out of the crack in the rock. The grass grew with blades as wide and tall as three men. Ralph shot at me with fireballs in both hands.

The grass formed a large thick column. The column smashed Ralph in the face and he fell to the ground. It followed him and slithered around his neck like a snake strangling him. He struggled to break lose. The green grass was so wet, he couldn't burn it.

I lifted him high into the air above me. I regained my shield and looked straight at him. "This is for Jason," I mumbled, as I shot the shield right at his face. His head didn't move because of its grip around his neck, but I could tell he was severely injured. I flew up to him and caught the shield.

"And Chris, Christopher, Marissa, Isabella, and Alice," I hollered hitting him over and over again.

"You will die as Titus will, and all his Tellus. You are all abominations."

The grass disintegrated around his neck and he fell limp to the ground. He landed on the rock in a pile. He didn't move, hurt and scared. It looked as if he had no power. He was no longer in flames.

I came down fast with a seed in my fist for one last striking blow. As I came down, his hand caught mine as his hand was on fire. It scorched my hand, as I tried to break free. His other hand stretched out and grabbed my neck. He lifted me off the ground. He raised me high into the air. I couldn't breath as my neck was burning. I had never experienced such pain as blood poured down my neck. I felt as if I were melting. I could smell my own flesh burning. I coughed. I wanted to fight back, I had to do something, but I struggled for air.

Ralph shot towards the ground, and he dragged me while he was flying against the rock. My head clashed against the rock. Dizziness and concussion struck me. My body went limp. I felt my skin scraping off as he dragged me. I felt as bone scraped rock. Blood spilled from my back. My eyes burned as he smashed me over and over. I caught sight of a tree below us.

It shot towards him, but he formed a staff of scorching fire and split it in half. Ralph punched me, and I dropped to the ground. I could barely move my neck, but I had to. I needed to stop him, to fulfill my destiny. Ralph floated to the ground. He turned back to normal. I saw blurs of him.

Ralph spoke, "You will never be like me. You can try, but I will murder you."

I tried getting up, but he kicked me hard. I lost my breath, but I could feel myself healing as he spoke.

"Stay down."

I concentrated my power and focused all my strength to this task. I closed my eyes and reached out to all of the plants and seeds. I could sense them and feel their potential as I called them. Blackness filled my vision as I searched for more power.

My arms stretched out into the air. Plants began to rise from the jungle floor. I could hear as all plants ripped out of the jungle floor. They all rose high into the air and shot towards the mountain at once. A thick tree wrapped around Ralph, again and again and again-forming a thick cocoon. I held him, high suspended in the air. The plants hit the mountain with such a force that it cracked.

I rose into the air with a seed in my hand. Ralph rolled around trying to escape his living tomb. Every plant in sight was pulling from the ground and striking at the mountains core. Rocks erupted and fell down the face into the reservoir. The mountain quaked and shook. Boulders rolled. I felt the vibrations moving through the air. The sound of the mayhem shattered my eardrums. Vibrations caused avalanches all along the mountain face.

I shot the log Ralph was entombed in into the center of the mountain. I concentrated and forced the plants in the earth to vibrate. The mountain shook more as boulders the size of buildings broke free and pummeled down the mountain, like leaves in the wind. I shook as I caused the destruction. My vision blurred. I dropped to a ledge on the side of the mountain to regain my strength.

I tried to stop the mayhem, but the vibrations continued and increased. The whole mountain shook. The sound was still blaring in my ears while the mountain rocked.

I was being tossed around like a pebble. Something was coming. A giant paw slammed down on the granite mountain-top causing the whole mountain to quake. A huge roar pierced my ears as the beast walked closer. The Magnificent Sphinx roared as sit stood on the mountaintop.

Suddenly, a hand grabbed me from behind. It burned my neck again as Ralph rose with me in the air. He had burned free in all the chaos. I should have been more focused I thought.

The sphinx roared, "**I TOLD YOU THAT I WOULD COME BACK BOY, IF YOU CAUSED MORE MAYHEM.**"

"What the heck is that?" asked Ralph.

Ralph lit my shirt on fire and shot me towards its mouth. I resisted with the seeds on my hands. We slowed still moving toward the beast's mouth. Fire burnt all around me. I cringed as my skin peeled rapidly like a snake. I shook. My eyes felt like they would explode. My mouth watered. Sweat poured down like rain. Consciousness was being drained from my mind.

I felt the tooth of the sphinx scrape across my chest **opening a deep wound.** I still had the seed. In a massive effort through the flames, I jerked Ralph backward and rolled him over in the air directly in front of the Sphinx. I swung my hand at his mouth palm open and delivered the seed dead center to his open mouth.

I kicked free from him and smiled "This is gonna hurt."

I closed my eyes. He tried to scream but immediately a thousand branches burst from his chest wrapping around and through him with apples growing on its deadly branches. His fire turned to smoke as he changed for the last time to his lifeless human form. I shot him towards the Sphinx's mouth as I let myself fall.

It snapped on Ralph and he disappeared. The sphinx's paw shot towards me. I saw it in time and shot away as it ran towards me.

"YOU BOY HAVE WRONGED ME!" it spoke.
The ground shook as The Great Sphinx darted. I was shooting back and forth at magnificent speeds. I didn't know how far I had gone.

The sphinx was large and fast and suddenly I felt the tooth of The Great Sphinx on my arm. My arm bled badly as it cut my arm to the bone. My arm felt tingly and I felt my bones almost cracking. It snapped its jaws, but I darted away the other direction. Finally, as I blacked out, I flew straight up hoping to the get out of the Sphinx's reach. I flew higher and higher as consciousness finally left my mind.

Chapter Nineteen

The next day I woke up early. Somehow, someone had collected me and got me back to the partially demolished training facility. Jack met me as I walked outside. Looking out at the top of the mountain it looked like there had been a war. I was so busy fighting I hadn't realized the destruction we had caused.

"What happened?" I asked

"You killed Ralph and then almost escaped the Sphinx. You suddenly started to fall. You were above the lake so I was able to swoop in and catch you. The Sphinx insisted I let him have you so he could kill you. I explained what Ralph was trying to do and that you had killed him to save the rest of us. When I said that, the Sphinx turned and mumbled something about "He is destined for great things," and walked away until he disappeared into the mountain.

We talked for hours about the last few weeks and what had happened. We spent the rest of the morning talking to the other kids from Ralph's side and trying to make sure they could get along. That afternoon we decided we would rebuild on the top of the mountain. The place was destroyed and was going to need a lot of work.

The next day started with sitting and considering what to do first. I decided to start with rebuilding the mansion. While I worked, I thought a lot about killing Ralph. That day would always be in my mind. I regretted killing him because he was my brother. I felt a mixture of emotions guilt, anguish, grief, happiness, and I didn't exactly know what I was supposed to feel.

For a few days we worked repairing things and changing them, so we would be able to survive well on the island. I kept watching, expecting Titus to appear any moment.

Today was cold and stormy, about three days after the battle. Rain poured down and thunder boomed overhead. The sky grew dark. The air was moist, and the wind was blowing hard.

I was off in the valley that used to be a jungle. I had left very early to try to repair some of the damage I had done. Grass had started to grow with all the rain, but the plants had been ripped out and slammed into the mountain side. There were mounds of trees and bushes everywhere. The ground was like a blast zone and only a few plants still grew in the **barren valley**. I was practicing with my abilities.

All the plants were stuck into the mountain. I pulled them out in groups and moved them down to the valley floor. I kept them suspended in the air and spaced them out, so they were ready for planting. I focused and forced all their roots to grow right before I punched them into the soft soil. I moved from area to area retrieving the plants and restoring the forest.

Rain beat down on me most of the day as I did this. Rain wasn't a big deal to me. I had never done this before, but I could feel the plants coming back to life.

I got lost in thought. I didn't know how long I would be here, but I considered that it might be a long time. I couldn't carry every person off the island even with Jack. What would happen if we lost power in the middle of a transport? Maybe someday when we had more control. I planted another large group of palm trees with a giant thump as they shot their roots into the soil.

There used to be a river bed here. I looked back up to the mountain and I saw a large crack in the granite at the top of the ridge. There was a large mound of trees and boulders that blocked the river. They had landed there during the battle and the water was backing up into a lake on the back side of the ridge. I ripped all the trees from the mound at once. Immediately the boulders started rolling down the mountain to the valley floor. I quickly planted the trees in the valley and watched as the water poured out over the ridge. The river found its path through the valley in a ferocious wall of water washing trees and mud with it as it moved.

I was hovering about 100 feet in the air, so I could watch the spectacle when I saw the flashes in the sky. I froze as the sky lit and then thunder boomed. I gazed at the sky, with the sound of rain and thunder piercing my ears.

Titus and lightning made me nervous, so I decided to go back and check on the others. I called up some seeds just in case and started flying towards the falls. Wind rushed into my face as I flew just off the water's edge up the waterfall. I landed softly on top of the granite rock at the edge of the falls.

Then, I heard a strange noise. A light lit in the dark sky. A lightning bolt was moving through the air. It curved and sped toward the ground, and hit the granite, about ten feet ahead of me. The granite cracked below the lightning bolt. Fragments of rock skidded across the granite top.

The lightning bolt hovered upright in front of me. I heard sound coming from inside the space and I could barely look at it because it burned my eyes. A silhouette was standing there behind the light.

I flashed my shield. Water was splashing on both of us. I was ready to attack. I knew this was Titus. The fact that he came in the form of lightning confirmed it. I fumbled the seed in my hand and made it grow into a sword (Another day, another battle.)

The lightning bolt disappeared. A boy now stood in its place. He looked much older than me, but he did not look as old as Titus. He was built like Titus. He had my brown wavy hair and muscles everywhere. He bore sea-blue eyes like Jack. He wore long black socks and gray shorts with a blue t-shirt.

I spoke intimidatingly, "I will kill you right here and now. Just give up."

The boy chuckled, "You think I'm Titus, don't you?"

"Oh, don't trick me, you psychopath."

I spun my shield and slashed it towards his shoulder. He shot a bolt of electricity towards me. It hit me in the shoulder and threw me backwards. I spun into the blow and caught myself on one knee as I slid backwards to a stop. Blood came from my burnt shoulder but that pain no longer bothered me. I pulled seeds out of the soil and watched to see what he would do.

Instead of attacking he reached in his bag and pulled out a device. He looked at me and slowly walked towards me. He held a device smaller than my hand. He pressed a blue button on the device. Blue lines flashed on me.

I immediately felt better. My shoulder healed instantly and even the burnt skin on my neck from my battle stopped burning. I felt amazing.

The kid reached out his hand. I grabbed his hand, and he pulled me up.

"So, you don't know who I am?"

"You are the boy in my dream. You shocked me in an alleyway," I answered.

The boy ruffled his hands through his hair, "I am your brother, Trent," he said

"Wait, what? You are telling me I have four brothers. Are you going to tell me I have six sisters too? Why are you here?" I demanded

"To get you, and no you have no more siblings," Trent exclaimed, "oh, except I forgot your ten other brothers," he laughed

"Haha, how did you know I was here?" I asked.

"I put a tracker in your ear," he said

"I have a lot of questions that Titus didn't answer."

"Did he try to kill you?"

"No, he was afraid of me. He wanted Ralph to do it," I insisted

"And, where is he?" he asked

"Where is who?"

"Ralph," he answered.

"Inside the belly of a Sphinx," I whispered.

Trent asked, "What did you say?"

I spoke clearer, "I shot him into the belly of a Sphinx."

"There is a Sphinx here?" he asked amazed.

"Yeah," I said

"As amazing as standing in the cold rain is, is there someplace else we can talk?"

"Oh yeah, let's go inside."

I grabbed my shield, and I led Trent towards the mansion. I walked through the doorway, then I closed it. The living room was empty as we walked through to my new room. My room was in the back all the way to the right and under the stairs. I sat down on the bed; he sat down on a chair on the opposite side of the room.

"I see you have grown in power," Trent began.

"I think so," I responded

"I made the holder for the gem. Well, I had a friend make it," Trent said

"Titus told me the story of my powers being taken away," I added

"Did he tell you he was the one that had your powers taken away by his associates? He made the pods that shot you out here? Did he tell you how big a traitor he is?"

"No, but I have a lot of questions. Like, why, just why were my other powers taken away?" I asked

"No," he informed emphatically

"What are my other powers?" I queried.

"I can't tell you. Trust me I would, but grandpa who has the powers from the same Imperium Stone, is afraid. He doesn't want you to end up like Titus. Titus was his prodigy, then he turned," he shared

"How did our father die?" I asked.

Jason looked at me oddly. It looked as though I angered him. His eyes filled with water. His chin quivered, and Trent's face went pale.

"I am so sorry that you have the burden of Ralph. He was the main reason you guys were put out here. He followed Titus."

"I know," I responded.

"How?" he asked.

I responded, "I have dreams. The dreams feel too real to be just dreams. I think they are my past."

"Is that probable Cole?" Trent asked as if someone else was in the room.

"Are you talking to someone else?" I asked.

"Sorry yeah," Trent responded. "We have microscopic transmitters like the one I put in your ear."

"Wait, does that mean you have been talking to me? Or where you talking to him?"

"You," he said

"Where are you going to take me?" I asked.

"To the place you belong?" he answered.

"And where is that, jail? I'm pretty sure I committed murder."

"Home," he responded.

"Will I meet Mom?"

"Maybe on the way, but now we are going to Mellontikos, to the school of the Meta's."

"Mellonta what?" I asked.

"Mellontikos is Greek for future."

"We are going to school?" I asked, moaning.

"Trust me, this won't be like school. They will use chips to load the information you would learn in a human school. The chips will load that information into our brains, but we will remember it like it's our own memory. The rest of the classes are all about using your powers and every other day we have school except Sunday and we have school on Saturday."

"What is it like?" I asked.

"Beyond anything you will ever see. Our grandpa actually made the school. Someone told him to build it. He is a true hero to all Metas.

"What is your power again?" I asked

"Well, all Metas have supernatural healing, but the power I have is lightning, and it is rare."

"Awesome," I responded. Little sparks came from Trent's palm.

"You really can't tell me my power?" I asked.

"I am sorry George. I would if I could. I know you will not turn, but it is for your own good."

"Okay," I responded.

"You are a good person George. It must have been so difficult and crazy."

"No, I am not. I let so many innocent people die. You don't even know what it was like."

My eyes swelled. My lip quivered. I had always tried to avoid the emotion of all this but expressing everything to Trent was great.

"Sorry man," he spoke.

"It's okay. It's all Titus's fault, mixed with Ralph's stubbornness."

"It will be much easier where we are going," Trent spoke.

"Well, aren't I destined to murder Titus."

"Yes, that is the first part of the prophecy," he responded.

"Wait, there is another part?"

Trent murmured, "Okay, the first few questions I was okay with. I ain't gonna explain your entire life though."

"So, it should be much easier than this, at the school."

Trent retorted, "Oh yes it will be, but maybe not for you."

"Thanks for cheering me up," I spoke

"How has Jack taken this experience?"

I responded, "Well, we three were born only a few months ago. We had to learn how to live. After learning how to live it felt normal."

Trent responded, "Well yeah, but how did he handle the death and the chaos."

I answered, "I thought Jack was dead until just like a few weeks ago."

"How?" asked Trent.

I responded, "One night I woke up to footsteps. I wandered through the rainforest. I fought a giant snake, then Ralph took us to the top of a mountain and almost killed me. They threw Jack off the waterfall."

"That sucks. He was alone all that time."

"He saved me," I spoke.

"So, I want to know the full story," Trent told me.

"Okay then…." I talked for what seemed like hours. Even though Trent had not been through this, he acted as if he knew what I was talking about. It was great to be in his presence. I had hope for the future. I knew things would be all right. Just letting out all the emotion and every trial I had been through felt great.

I shared every little detail about everything I remembered. I had never felt so at ease. I just relaxed and talked.

When I was done talking, Trent spoke, "Let's go see Jack, shall we."

"Yeah," I responded. We walked out of my room and into the main living room. Jack was the only one person in the living room.

He saw me, and his eyes filled with rage. He clenched his fists. He was very angry and walked towards me. As he got closer, he jumped up and punched Trent in the face.

"You like that Titus. Oh, let's have some fun. I'm gonna rip you to shreds and after that, I am gonna."

I stopped Jack by blurting, "This is our brother Trent. He isn't Titus."

Jack took deep breaths, "I'm sorry," he spoke.

"Thanks," Trent added.

"Again, I'm, sorry. I've never seen him before and George said he was expecting him to come fight," Jack answered.

"No problem. I get beat up all the time."

"George, could I speak to Jack alone?" Trent asked

"Yes," I responded and walked away.

I walked towards the rock-climbing wall. All the kids were now in the room waiting to climb. We all picked a route and started climbing. Getting to the top was hard. I had designed this wall, so it would always be a challenge. I had to use all my upper body strength. My muscles tightened and spasmed as I climbed.

We competed to see who could get to the highest point. I was light and strong and this time I won the climb. Elijah was the biggest, and he didn't get up that far. Strengths are not always an advantage I thought.

We did this challenge over and over. Sometimes, I lost and sometimes I won. Chloe was also light, so she was my competition. Arthur was always joking as we climbed. He made me fall many times. We were kids again for a moment lost in insignificant things.

After what felt like hours of competing, Jack and Trent came back.

"Don't fall," Trent yelled.

I laughed. I could not control myself, lost my grip, and fell to the ground.

"Thanks for ruining my record," I thanked sarcastically.

"Your welcome," **Trent** responded.

Jack whispered, "We've got to go."

"What about them," I whispered back.

"**Trent** will send people to come get them."

"Okay."

Jack got them all together and explained. They were all very excited.

We walked over to the middle of the living room. We stood in an open area. Trent reached into his bag and threw a small steel contraption down on the floor directly in front of us. There was a whir and then a flash of light.

"So where now?" Jack asked.

Trent responded, "Home," and we dissolved.

Acknowledgments

I'd like to thank my family and friends for their support and encouragement throughout the process. Their feedback kept me going and helped me stay focused on my goals.

Thanks to Olena Kalashnik for going above and beyond my standards for the illustrations and being patient with me.

Thanks to the designers of Pro-Writing Aid for developing and maintaining a website with a great purpose.

Many thanks to my father for proofing the manuscript and giving feedback over the many months of writing. No one could have been more helpful or given more honest feedback.

Finally, thanks to my brothers for loving a great story as much as I do.

About the Author

Alex Henry is the author of <u>No Man's Island</u> and is an avid reader and writer of Science Fiction. Alex is the middle of 5 brothers and spends his time in a diverse range of activities.

At the age of 12 he is the progenitor of a 2017 patented "Product of the Year" and new home technology, plays competitive basketball, loves creating, building, learning, and writing.

Alex does his writing at home in sunny Northern California. He intends to extend the series to a five volume, set and hopes to accomplish that by the time he is 18.

He is a humble overachiever with big ideas for the future.

18915987R00151

Made in the USA
San Bernardino, CA
21 December 2018